For [illegible] forty years
Yearling has been the leading name
in classic and award-winning literature
for young readers.

Yearling books feature children's
favorite authors and characters,
providing dynamic stories of adventure,
humor, history, mystery, and fantasy.

Trust Yearling paperbacks to entertain,
inspire, and promote the love of reading
in all children.

For more than forty years,
Yearling has been the leading name
in classic and award-winning literature
for young readers.

Yearling books feature children's
favorite authors and characters,
providing dynamic stories of adventure,
humor, history, mystery, and fantasy.

Trust Yearling paperbacks to entertain,
inspire, and promote the love of reading
in all children.

OTHER YEARLING BOOKS BY LOIS LOWRY YOU WILL ENJOY

ANASTASIA AT THIS ADDRESS

ANASTASIA HAS THE ANSWERS

ANASTASIA'S CHOSEN CAREER

ANASTASIA AGAIN!

ANASTASIA AT YOUR SERVICE

ANASTASIA ON HER OWN

ANASTASIA, ASK YOUR ANALYST

ANASTASIA KRUPNIK

ATTABOY, SAM!

SEE YOU AROUND, SAM!

all about Sam

LOIS LOWRY

Illustrated by Diane deGroat

A YEARLING BOOK

Published by Yearling, an imprint of Random House Children's Books
a division of Random House, Inc., New York

Visit us on the Web! www.randomhouse.com/kids

Educators and librarians, for a variety of teaching tools, visit us at
www.randomhouse.com/teachers

ISBN: 0-440-40221-2

Reprinted by arrangement with Houghton Mifflin Company

Printed in the United States of America

November 1992

40 39 38 37 36 35 34 33 32

For Jamie,
who is very much like Sam

all about Sam

1

It had certainly been an exciting morning for him, but a confusing one, too. There were bright lights, which he didn't like, and he was cold, and someone was messing around with his belly button, which hurt.

And he didn't know who he was yet.

"A fine healthy boy," he heard someone say. But that told him only *what* he was, not who.

He squinted and wiggled and stuck his tongue out, and they all laughed. He liked the sound of the laughter, so he did it again, and they all laughed some more.

Then they put some clothes on him, which made him nice and warm, though the clothes felt odd because he had never worn clothes before.

They passed him around from one person to

another, which was a little scary because he was afraid they might drop him.

"Don't drop me," he wanted to say. But it came out sounding like "Waaaahhhh." Someone said "Shhhh" in a soft voice and patted his back gently.

"Who *am* I?" he wanted to ask, but that sounded like "Waaaahhhh" again, and she simply patted his back once more.

Finally they put him down in a little bed and dimmed the lights.

He opened his eyes wide now that the lights weren't so bright, but he couldn't see much: just the sides of the little bed, and high above him the blurred faces of people.

It was all too confusing and exhausting. He sighed, closed his eyes, and went to sleep.

When he woke again, he was in a different place. He was still in the little bed, but the bed had been moved; he knew because the walls were green instead of white. Now there were fewer people — fewer faces looking down at him. He could see these people a little better because his eyes weren't quite so new, so he blinked to focus more clearly and stared up at them.

There was a woman, and he could tell that he

liked her a lot. She had happy eyes and a nice smile, and when she bent closer and touched his cheek with her finger, it was a gentle touch filled with love. He wiggled with happiness.

Then the woman's face went away, and a man leaned down. The man seemed to have his head on upside down; there was hair on the chin, but none on the head. Maybe that was the way men were supposed to look. The man had a nice smile, too.

Finally, a girl leaned over the bed. She had hair the same color as the man's chin hair, and she wore glass over her eyes, which were interesting to look at. But she wasn't smiling. She had a suspicious look.

The girl stared at him for a long time. He stared back. Finally she reached in and touched his hand. He had his hand curled up because he hadn't yet figured out anything interesting to do with it. But when the girl touched his hand, he grabbed her finger, which was just the perfect size for grabbing. He held on tight.

"Hey," the girl said, "I really like him!"

Of course you do, silly, he thought. He tried to say that, but only managed to spit and make a sound like "Phhhwww."

The man and the woman had happy smiles, which they aimed at the girl.

"Does he wet his diapers a whole lot?" the girl asked the man and the woman.

Yes, he thought, I do. As a matter of fact, I am wetting them right now, right at this very moment.

"He's only five hours old," the woman said. "So I haven't had time to conduct an exhaustive study. But in all honesty, Anastasia, I have to tell you that I think he will probably wet his diapers a whole lot."

You're right, he thought. I plan to. Because it feels good.

He yawned. They were talking to each other, but he didn't understand what they were saying, and he was a little bored. He was sleepy, too.

Then he heard the man say, "Have you picked out his name?"

And he heard the girl say, "Of *course* I've picked out his name."

So he tried hard to stay awake, even though he was sleepy, because he knew this was important. He blinked and yawned and wiggled and wet his diapers a little more, and waited. He waited while they murmured things to each other, which he couldn't hear. Then, one by one, they leaned over his bed again.

The girl with the pieces of glass over her eyes peered in at him, and now she was smiling. "Hi,

Sam," she said.

The woman with the gentle voice looked down, and *she* said, "Hi, Sam."

The man with his head on upside down leaned close. In his deep, pleasant voice, he said, "Hi, Sam."

Oh, he thought happily. Now I understand. This is my family. My sister, my mother, my father.

And I am Sam, he thought and liked the sound of it.

Sam.

Sam.

SAM.

Sam was glad when they told him they were taking him home, because the word *home* sounded kind of nice, especially the way they said it to him in warm, happy voices.

But he hated the hat.

He didn't mind the dry diapers — by now, after three days, he was quite accustomed to getting dry diapers. He liked the chance to kick his legs in the air while they changed him, and he loved the soft feeling of the powder they sprinkled on his bottom.

He didn't mind the nightgown, though he

hated it when they remembered to fold the mitten part over his hands. It was much better when they left the mitten turned back, because on each hand he had fingers and a thumb that he liked to suck when he was bored, or if they didn't feed him quite quickly enough when he was hungry.

But today, for the first time, they put a sweater on top of the nightgown, and the sweater was scratchy. I don't like this, he thought.

Then they put on the hat. And he *hated* the hat. It hurt under his chin where they tied it, and one of his ears was folded right in half inside the hat. He found the edge of the hat with one hand and tried to pull it off. They laughed and covered his hand with that terrible mitten.

I HATE THIS HAT, he yelled. But it sounded like "Waaahhhh," and they all said "Shhhhhh" and patted his back.

I HATE THIS HAT, he yelled again, and they jiggled him up and down and kissed his cheek.

"We're going home," they said.

NOT WITH THIS HAT ON, Sam yelled, but they didn't pay any attention to him, none at all. They wrapped a thick blanket around him, carried him through some doorways, down some halls, through some more doorways, and down some more halls.

It was about a hundred and fifty-three miles

that they carried him, and for the entire distance he yelled, TAKE THIS HATEFUL HAT OFF ME!

But they didn't.

Then, suddenly, they went through one more doorway, and they were outside. It was cold and it was windy, and Sam had never felt anything like that before. He closed his eyes tight and snuggled down into the blanket as far as he could. The man held him very close, and he could feel the man's jacket against his cheek. Only his nose and his closed eyes were sticking out of the blanket, and he could feel the cold wind on those parts of him. But he was warm everyplace else — even his head.

Okay, he thought; you guys know best. I guess I *need* this hat.

He liked the car. Its sound was interesting, and he especially liked the feel of it as it moved. He thought he might even fall asleep. But he stayed awake because the girl, his sister, Anastasia, was holding him now, and she didn't hold him as firmly as his father did. She wasn't used to him yet. He was afraid she might drop him.

Hold me tighter, he said. A little firmer arm under the head and neck, please. But it sounded like spitting noises, and she smiled down at him and giggled.

"Look, Sam," she said. "Look out the window. There's a big oak tree. It doesn't have any leaves yet, but it will, soon."

He tried to look, but the oak tree was too far away and the car was moving too fast.

"Now look, Sam," Anastasia said. "That's a maple tree. We're at the corner of our street."

She pointed, and he cringed. Please put that arm back under my bottom, he thought. And she did.

His sister moved him back and forth in her arms gently, and she sang to him. "Rock-a-bye, baby," she sang, "in the treetop . . ."

Oak tree, he thought. Maple tree. Treetop. *Trees* must be something important.

When they got home, he knew he was right. The man — his father — carried him into the house while his sister and mother walked beside him.

"Sam," his sister was saying in an eager, excited voice, "we just have a small apartment. And there wasn't an extra bedroom for you. So we fixed one up in the pantry. We painted the walls blue, and we put your little crib in there, and we took the dishes out of the cupboards and put your clothes in there, and Mom made curtains with unicorns on them just for you. I bet you're the only baby in Cambridge who gets to sleep in a pantry!"

Pan tree, thought Sam. Rock-a-bye, baby, in the pan tree. Okay. Whatever it means, I'm all for it, because she said "sleep." And I am very, very sleepy.

They laid him down in the crib, and the woman changed his diapers. She used the same soft powder that he loved. Then she took off his sweater and, *finally* — about *time* — she took off his hat.

He took a quick look around the pan tree, wiggled down beneath the blanket they put over him, yawned, found a finger to suck on, and closed his eyes.

2

At first he slept a lot. He couldn't think of anything else to do. The pan tree was pleasant enough, but it was kind of boring. Sometimes they took him out of his bed there and carried him around. That was always fun, because he got to look at different stuff, and his eyes were starting to work pretty well now.

He especially liked the rocking chair in the living room. His mom took him there to feed him, and sometimes he got so interested in listening to the squeak of the chair and looking at the pictures on the walls that he forgot to eat. Later, in his crib in the pan tree, he would think: I forgot to eat. Now I'm hungry.

So he would yell, I FORGOT TO EAT,

AND NOW I'M HUNGRY. It sounded like "Waaaahhhhh," and he had improved his voice so that it was quite loud now.

When he yelled that, his mom would come. She would stand there looking down at him, and she would say, "Are you hungry *again*?" in an amazed voice.

Sam would say, IT'S BECAUSE I WAS LOOKING AT THE PICTURES ON THE WALLS, AND I FORGOT TO EAT! which sounded like a very long, very loud "Waaaaahhhhh." And his mom would sigh and take him back to the rocking chair and feed him again. She was a pretty good sport about it, except in the middle of the night, when occasionally she grumbled a little. And once, in the middle of the night, she fell sound asleep in the rocking chair. Her arms became limp and Sam had to say "WAAAAAAAHHHH" very loudly — more loudly than usual — because he was afraid she would drop him on the floor.

He wasn't often worried about that though, not the way he had been at first. No one ever dropped him. Not even when they gave him a bath and he was wet and slippery with soap. They held him good and tight. Even Anastasia had learned to hold him tight.

Sometimes Anastasia took him outside for a

walk. He liked being out in his carriage because he got to look at trees and their moving leaves. The pan tree had no leaves, which was puzzling (he thought the pan tree was very weird compared to the outside trees), but finally they hung something over his crib. It had colorful things dangling from it, and if he bounced in the crib, the colorful things moved. He liked to look at that now and then — for about two minutes, no more. After that it was boring. When it got boring, he yelled, I AM BORED WITH LOOKING AT THIS THING OVER MY CRIB, which was a slightly different sort of "Waaaahhhhh."

The only bad thing about going outside was that dumb hat. They always put the hat on him when they took him outside, and they wouldn't take it off, not even when he yelled I HATE THIS HAT for a long time. So he concentrated on getting his hands to work better. Any day now he would be able to take that hat off; and when he mastered that, he would never *ever* wear that hat again.

There was a whole lot of stuff to learn, and it took a while. First he had learned to bounce himself in his crib, so that the hanging thing would move and be interesting for two minutes.

Next, there was the whole diaper-changing

thing. After the soft-feeling powder got sprinkled on his bottom, which he liked so much that he always smiled — and they *loved* it when he smiled — then his mom would put the dry diaper on. Then — this was the best part — before she pulled his nightgown down, she would lean forward, put her face on his tummy, and go "Blurble blurble" with her mouth, which tickled so much that he would laugh out loud.

But when his dad or his sister changed his diaper, they didn't know that they were supposed to do the blurble blurble thing. So he had to teach them.

He taught them by yelling DO THE BLURBLE BLURBLE THING, which sounded like "Waaahhhh," after they changed him.

Then they would say, "Why does he always cry when we change him?" as if their feelings were hurt.

"I don't know," his mom would say in a puzzled voice.

IT'S BECAUSE THEY DON'T DO BLURBLE BLURBLE, he yelled, but they didn't understand him.

Finally — it seemed to take forever — one day, his mom said, "I bet I know!" And she explained to them about the blurble blurbling.

Sometimes they still forgot, but he reminded them each time, and they were learning.

Now and then they left him all alone, lying on a blanket on the living room floor. He wished they would hang around and make faces at him, but he understood that they had other stuff to do sometimes. And he liked the time on the blanket. He kicked his legs a lot and looked at the living room stuff. The curtains were nice, and the pictures on the walls were interesting, and sometimes they even left the TV on and he liked the voices of the TV people, though not as well as he liked his family's voices.

One day, when he was alone on the blanket on the living room floor, he leaned hard on his side and pushed with his arm. Arms were great pushers, he had discovered recently. He could use one arm to push away the spoon when his mom tried to make him eat oatmeal, which tasted disgusting.

"Sam, stop that!" his mom would say when he pushed the spoon away. So he would answer, OATMEAL IS DISGUSTING, which was a wonderful thing to say with his mouth full, because it sounded like "Phhllllt" and made oatmeal fly out of his mouth and onto his clothes. Then he could grab it with his hand and put it into his hair, which felt good. Even though he hated oatmeal, it was always fun to be *fed* oatmeal because he could smear it around and push the spoon and stuff, and sometimes it meant he even got a second bath, which he liked.

But on this particular day, lying on the floor, he wasn't thinking about oatmeal. He was thinking about his arm and about how it pushed.

He pushed harder and harder, leaning on his arm, and suddenly his whole body tipped over. He had started out on his tummy, and now he was on his back. He had also gotten a clunk on the head, but he didn't even care about that because it was so interesting, what pushing would do.

He began to wiggle and push again. It was harder, starting from his back, but he worked on it for quite a long time, until suddenly: clunk. He had done it agan, and now he was on his tummy, but he was off the blanket.

Now he was on the living room rug, a place he had never been before.

He tasted the rug. Yuck. The rug tasted terrible, much worse than oatmeal; but that didn't matter because he wasn't hungry anyway. Sam was on a roll.

Lean. Push. Push. Up, up, up, and: clunk. He was over again. He was heading for the big green chair in the corner.

Now he was getting better at it. It didn't take so long each time. Clunk: tummy. Clunk: back. He wished that he didn't clunk his head each time. Tomorrow, maybe, he would concentrate on the head part.

There: he was at the chair. One more roll would do it. He pushed with his arm, raised his behind, leaned, and clunk. He was *under* the green chair, exactly where he wanted to be.

He lay there very quietly, looking up at the underside of the chair, where a metal thing poked out, and there were some dangling threads that were much more interesting than the thing that hung over his crib in the pan tree.

He could hear footsteps. He knew they were Anastasia's footsteps. Hers were noisy, and they had dangling shoelaces flapping, unlike his mom's softer steps or his dad's firm, big ones.

Sam waited. He smiled, waiting, under the green chair.

Then the footsteps stopped — they were quite close to him — and he heard Anastasia scream. "Mom! Sam's gone!"

He heard his mom's soft footsteps coming very fast. He waited quietly, smiling to himself.

"He was here ten minutes ago!" he heard Anastasia say. "He's been kidnapped! Someone climbed in the window and stole him!"

"That's impossible," he heard his mom say in a worried voice.

Anastasia wailed, "He's been kidnapped! Someone climbed in the window and stole him! Look for a ransom note!"

"Don't be foolish," his mom's voice said, but it sounded very nervous.

"Here! Here's a ransom note, right here on the desk! You read it, Mom. I can't bear to. It says steak, right at the top. They'll return Sam if we give them steak. Read it, and then call the FBI immediately."

"That's my grocery list," Mom said. "Don't be ridiculous. Is your dad home? Did he come in the back door, and I didn't notice? Myron? Are you home? Do you have Sam?"

"Mom!" Anastasia begged. "*Do* something!"

Under the chair, Sam grinned. He had never caused such a commotion before, not even the night last week when his ear ached and he cried for a whole hour.

He watched their feet, and he listened to their voices with interest. Finally, he laughed out loud, pushed hard with his arm, leaned, and rolled out from under the chair.

Anastasia and Mom burst out laughing. Mom knelt, picked him up, said "Silly old Sam," and blurble blurbled into his neck, mixing the blurbles with kisses.

Gotcha, Sam thought with delight.

Sam was frustrated.

He couldn't make them understand what he was saying. His mouth didn't work right. He would try very hard to call politely to them, "I want my diaper changed," or "I woke up from my nap and I am very lonely here in the pan tree," but it always came out sounding like "Waahhh."

Or he would try to say, "Another spoonful of those mushed-up peaches-and-tapioca, please," but it would sound like "Phhhhfft," and the peaches-and-tapioca in his mouth would fly out and wind up on his stomach and his feet.

He could understand what *they* said. Every word. At least, he could understand what his family said: his mom, his dad, and Anastasia, his sister.

Strangers were something different. They spoke another language, apparently. Strangers sometimes leaned over his crib or his carriage and said things like "Ba-ba, boo-boo" or "kootchy kootchy," and none of that made any sense at all, so he just smiled politely or stared at them with a puzzled look.

Once — only once — did it come out right. His mom had been feeding him, and it was strained apricots, one of his favorites. He wanted more. Lots more, right away. While he was trying to say that, but saying "Phhhfft" instead, she gave him another spoonful. So Sam smiled and said thank you. And it worked. It sounded like "Tattoo," but his mom understood, and she clapped her hands and called, "Myron! Anastasia! Come quickly!"

They came running, both of them, and Mom said, "Sam said 'thank you' when I gave him a bite of apricots!"

Dad and Anastasia both frowned and stared at Sam.

"Impossible," Dad said.

Sam wiggled around so that his little tilted chair bounced up and down. He waved his arms. He grinned. "I did! I really did!" he said. But it sounded like, "Blah, blah, blurb," and darn it all, he lost the whole bite of apricots, right down his bib.

"He really did," mom said.

Dad and Anastasia both laughed. "Give us a break, Mom," Anastasia said, and she poked a finger in Sam's armpit for a tickle.

"Another few months, Katherine," Dad said. "*Then* he'll start talking."

Now another few months had passed. He had some teeth now. Sometimes he bit his own finger by mistake and it hurt. He tried not to do that. He tried to bite *other* people's fingers.

And he bit toys. His teddy bear wasn't good biting, because it was too soft; but there was a hard plastic pretzel that he chewed on quite a bit. And the bars on the side of his crib were made of wood; he gnawed on them while they thought he was sleeping.

Also when they thought he was asleep, he practiced talking. He liked to do it when no one was listening so they wouldn't laugh. "Ba, ba, ba," he practiced late at night, saying it quietly to himself in the dark.

"Ta, ta, ta" was a good one. And "Ma, ma, ma."

He could say "me, me, me" and "ho, ho, ho."

He could do body parts. In the middle of the night, if he woke up and was bored, he kicked his blanket off, lifted his legs in the air, pointed with his finger, and said softly, “Knee, knee, knee.” He had two of those.

“Eye, eye, eye,” he said and pointed. Ouch. He had two of those, too, but he had to be careful, pointing, because if he pointed too hard at his eyes, it hurt.

When he worked hard at it, he could put two sounds together and make “Nose.” He had only one nose, but it was fun to point at it, because sometimes he could poke his finger *into* it.

Nobody knew that he was practicing talking. It was his secret. He was going to let them know when the right moment came.

And in the meantime, he was working hard on some other stuff, too, at the other end of his body. Legs and feet, those things were called (he could say “feet” already, practicing at night). Feet also had toes — which he could say: “Tose, tose, tose” — but toes didn’t seem very useful. They certainly weren’t as handy as fingers, which could grab stuff, and pinch, and pull Anastasia’s hair.

But legs and feet were very useful because they could get you from here to there. Rolling did too, of course, but Sam had been rolling for quite a while now, and he was beginning to get bored with rolling. You couldn’t aim yourself very well and sometimes you rolled into the coffee table by mistake and whacked your nose. And when you rolled, you often got a mouthful of rug by mistake.

So he was practicing legs and feet. Using legs and feet, you could get yourself upright so that you looked like a real grown-up person. Once you were upright, like a grown-up, you never had to eat rug.

Now, finally, on a Saturday morning, he was ready to give the thing a try in front of the whole family. They were in the living room, all of them. Dad was lying on the couch, reading a newspaper. He had his shoes and socks off, and his big bare feet were propped on the arm of the couch. Mom was sitting in the green chair, knitting. She knit a lot. Knitting looked like an interesting thing to do with fingers. Sometimes, when she wasn't looking, Sam rolled over to her basket of knitting stuff and tried to knit. But she always grabbed it away from him and said, "No, no, no." *No* was an easy word to say. Sam said it a lot to himself at night, practicing. Soon he would say it to his family. He planned to say it often.

Anastasia was there, too. She was sitting on the floor barefoot, and she was painting her toenails bright red, using a tiny brush that went into a little bottle. A minute ago she had reached over very quietly and painted her father's biggest toenail bright red. He hadn't noticed yet.

No one was paying any attention to Sam. He was sitting on the rug chewing on his plastic pretzel.

Very quietly — just as stealthily as Anastasia had painted her dad's toenail — Sam put his pretzel down.

He reached over and put both hands firmly on the edge of the coffee table. He raised himself to his knees. Knee, he told himself. Knee.

Then he said — still to himself — foot. And he raised himself to one foot.

And again: foot. And he was on the other foot. He pushed hard. Now he was upright, the way he sometimes was in his crib, holding the sides.

That wasn't enough. He wanted to be upright on his own, like the grown-ups. So very carefully, very slowly, concentrating very hard, with his face in a frown, he let go with one hand.

It felt scary. A little wobbly. For an instant he touched the table again, just to steady himself. Then he took his hand away. Finally, he let go with the other hand.

He felt very tall, very brave. He stood there alone. No one was watching. Dad turned a page of the newspaper. Mom turned her knitters around and began knitting in the other direction. Anastasia dipped her little brush into the little bottle of toe paint again.

Sam eyed the distance from the table to the TV set. He thought about how to get there. Pick one foot up, put it down, pick the other foot up, put it down; then do the whole thing again, he thought.

He took off across the room, toward the TV. Halfway there, he stopped and called in a loud voice: "SEE ME? I'M *UP*!"

He heard his mother call, "Look! Sam's walking!"

He heard Anastasia shriek, "He's *talking*, too!"

He heard his father bellow, "What — in the name of — *what* is this on my toenail?"

Sam lost his balance. Splat. He landed on his diaper, and it was wet.

"Now," he said thoughtfully, "I'm down."

But he didn't mind being down, because he knew he could get back up. He knew he could walk to the TV, and he could reach the knobs and turn it on — *loud* — whenever he wanted. He could walk down the hall to the kitchen, when his mom wasn't looking, and open the cupboard under the sink and pull out the squeezy bottle of soap and squeeze it all smooshy on the floor — something he'd been wanting to do for a long

time. He could walk to the bathroom and unroll the interesting roll of paper that hung there on the wall. He could walk to Anastasia's room, and if his arms reached far enough — he was pretty certain they would — he could pull all the papers off her desk and crumple them into balls.

He could tip over all the wastebaskets. He could pull books out of the bookcases and tear their pages out. And if he yanked at the cords that hung down, he thought he could probably tip over lamps and make wonderful crashing noises.

Sam sat there in the middle of the living room and thought about the wonderful things that the future held for him as a walking person. Then he shifted himself to his knees.

Knee. Knee. Foot. Foot. Push. Up. Now he was upright again, and life was not going to be boring anymore. Now he was a real grown-up, and he hoped that soon they would get him some blue jeans like all grown-ups, so that he would never have to wear dumb baby overalls again.

"Here I go!" Sam said in a loud voice, and he was off and running.

3

"Where does the water go?" Sam asked, peering into the kitchen sink. He was standing on a chair, helping his mother wash dishes. She let him do only the plastic things, but it was fun, because he got to splash water around. He watched the water go down the drain with a gurgling sound.

"Into the pipes," Mom said. She dried him with a towel and helped him down to the floor.

Sam headed down the hall. It sure was fun, not being a baby anymore. Now that he was big, he could walk anywhere he wanted. He walked to his father's desk. Dad wasn't there. He was atwork.

Sam didn't know what *atwork* meant, except

that it meant Dad wasn't around. When Dad was atwork, he disappeared. When the door opened, and Dad appeared, carrying a briefcase, then he wasn't atwork anymore.

Anastasia was never atwork, though sometimes she was atschool. And Mom was never atwork. Only Dad.

Today, Dad was atwork, so no one was in the room where the desk was, and Sam went in. He climbed onto his dad's chair and twirled it around. That was always fun. Sometimes he twirled around so much he got dizzy, and once he had even tipped over.

But today he didn't want to do twirling. He stood carefully on the chair after it stopped twirling, and slithered across the big desktop on his tummy until he reached what he wanted. The pipes.

Dad had a whole row of pipes standing up in a rack. Sometimes he took one out and set it on fire and ate it for a while.

Mom had told Sam that the water went into the pipes.

Sam took out the first pipe and looked into the end to see the water. But there was no water there. He dropped the pipe on the floor.

He looked into each pipe, one by one. No water. He poked his fingers in the pipes. Some of them had little bits of brown stuff like cereal in them. He tasted that. Yuck.

He dropped all the pipes on the floor and went back to the kitchen.

"No water in the pipes," he announced.

Mom looked over at the sink. "No," she said. "I guess not. It's all gone."

Sam frowned. He wandered into the bathroom, twirled the roll of paper around, and decided he wouldn't unroll it right now — he had already done that once today. He pulled on the handle of the toilet.

Flush. Sam loved that sound.

Mom appeared in the doorway of the bathroom. She sighed.

Sam was watching the water rush around inside the toilet. "Where does *this* water go?" he asked. "Into the pipes, too?"

"That's right," Mom told him.

So he went back to look at the pipes again. This time Mom followed him. She started to laugh.

"Not these pipes, Sam," she said as she picked them up from the floor and put them back on Dad's desk. "The water goes into the special water pipes, and then it goes under the ground, and after a long, long time it ends up in the ocean, and then from the ocean it goes up into the air, and then it comes raining back down again, and into the lakes, and back into the pipes, and someday it comes back into our sink."

She picked Sam up, sat him on her lap, and tied his shoes. "Did you understand all of that?" she asked.

Sam grinned. He didn't really. But he said "Yep," and gave Mom a kiss on her neck.

Into the pipes. Into the ground. Into the ocean. Into the air. And then it rains down.

He had an idea. When Mom was back in the kitchen again, making dinner, Sam went into Mom and Dad's bedroom. If he pulled out the bottom drawer of the bureau, he could stand on it and see what was on the top. There was interesting stuff on the top, sometimes.

Today, on top of the bureau, Sam discovered a piece of Kleenex. That was boring. Then he saw a thing called a lipstick. Lipstick wasn't boring. You could open it up and then you could write with it. He had done that once; he had written with the lipstick on Mom and Dad's bedspread.

Mom hadn't liked that. She had said, "NO, NO, NO! *NEVER* DO THAT AGAIN, SAM!"

So he didn't do it again. He didn't even open the lipstick. But he took it from the top of the bureau and went to the bathroom.

Carefully he dropped it into the toilet. When he pulled the handle, he knew, it would go into the pipes, into the ground, into the ocean, into the air, and then it would rain down. Lipsticks would rain down. And *that* would be interesting.

He almost pulled the flushing handle. But first, he decided, he would add more stuff.

He dropped in his plastic pretzel. Now it would rain lipsticks and pretzels. But that wasn't enough.

Sam looked around. He could see something interesting on the side of the bathroom sink — Mom's earrings. He stood on tiptoes, reached the earrings, and added them.

One of his sneakers had come untied again and he pulled it off. Would it be interesting if sneakers rained down, with lipsticks and pretzels and earrings? Yes, Sam decided. So he dropped the sneaker into the toilet.

Now he was ready to flush.

Maybe, Sam thought suddenly, Mom would like to watch.

He went back to the kitchen. Mom was just putting something into the oven. "Hi, Sam," she said. "Are you getting into mischief?"

"Nope," Sam said.

"What happened to your shoe?" Mom asked.

Sam grinned. "Come see," he said. He tugged at her hand.

Mom followed him to the bathroom, and Sam

pointed, showing her the wonderful flush he was about to make.

"Oh, *no*!" Mom said in a loud voice. She reached in and pulled out the dripping sneaker. She pulled out the pretzel. Then the lipstick. Then the earrings. She dropped all of the wet things into the sink.

She knelt on the floor beside Sam. She gave him a kiss. "Sam," she said. "None of those things likes to be in water. Not shoes. Not toys. Not lipsticks. Not Mom's earrings. They don't want to be wet. Do you understand?"

Sam nodded.

"Promise you won't do it again?"

Sam promised, and Mom went back to the kitchen. He *did* understand. What he needed was something that *did* like to be wet.

He thought about Dad's big black umbrella. But he knew it wouldn't fit.

Then he thought of the perfect thing. He went to Anastasia's room and turned the wastebasket upside down so that he could stand on it and reach her goldfish bowl. Anastasia's goldfish was named Frank.

And Frank *loved* water. Sam knew that for sure, because once he had dumped Frank out, and Anastasia had screamed and grabbed Frank and filled the bowl with water again even before she mopped up the floor. "Frank *needs* water," she had explained to Sam. "Frank is very frightened and unhappy if he doesn't have water."

Carefully Sam dipped his plastic clown cup into the goldfish bowl. "Frank," he said, "you will be very happy."

He wished that Anastasia were home, instead of outside riding her bike, so that she could see how happy he was making Frank.

Frank floated very happily in the clown cup all the way to the bathroom.

He *loved* it in the toilet, because the toilet was bigger than the goldfish bowl. Sam watched him swim in the toilet for a long time.

Now, thought Sam, you get to go in the pipes. Under the ground. Into the ocean. Up to the sky.

And *then* you will rain back down.

He pulled the handle. "Yaaayyyy!" Sam shouted happily as he watched Frank spin and swirl.

He ran to the kitchen.

"I flushed Frank!" Sam announced.

He couldn't figure out why Mom wasn't happy about it. Dad, when he came home from atwork, wasn't happy, either. Worst of all, when Anastasia came in, Mom and Dad told her about it in very sad, quiet voices. And Anastasia began to cry.

That night, from his crib, looking through his window, Sam watched the sky. He waited and waited for it to rain goldfish so that he could give Frank back to his sister. But it never, ever did.

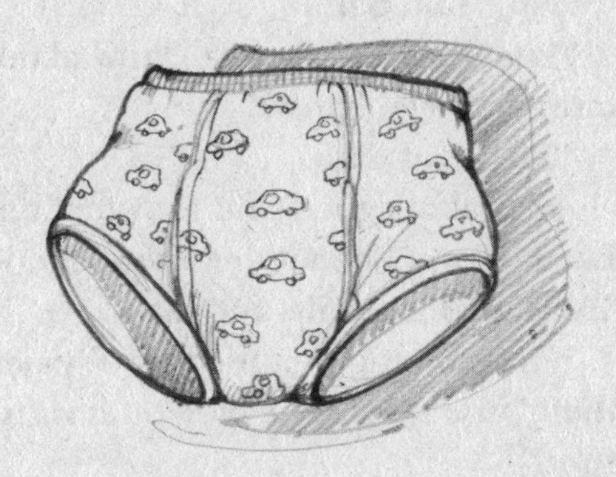

4

"Sam, I do wish you would be trained," his mother said one day as she was changing his diaper.

"No," said Sam. He said it very sweetly and smiled.

He didn't know what she meant. But he said no anyway. Sam liked saying no. It was an easier word to say than yes. And it always had a more interesting effect. When he said no, people sighed and frowned and scrunched their faces up. Sometimes his sister, Anastasia, got so mad that she shrieked when Sam said no.

Once, when Anastasia was getting Sam dressed for bed, she asked him, "Do you want to wear these pajamas, Sam? The ones with teddy bears on them?" She held them up.

"No," said Sam.

"Well," said Anastasia, "how about these? The ones with elephants?"

"No," said Sam.

Anastasia sighed and frowned and scrunched her face up. Soon, Sam knew, she would shriek. He waited, happily, for that.

His sister got another pair of pajamas. "These, then," she said. "The blue ones with a hole in the foot."

"No," Sam said loudly.

Then she shrieked. "MOM! Sam says no to *everything*!"

His mother was scrubbing the bathtub and picking up all the boats that Sam had been sailing during his bath. "Of course he does," she told Anastasia. "He's in the middle of the Terrible Twos."

Sam looked around himself with interest. He didn't see Terrible Twos anyplace. He was in the middle of the room, standing there wearing his Pampers.

He didn't know what his mother was talking about half the time. He was in the middle of the apartment. He was in the middle of the *rug*. Soon he would be in the middle of his crib. How could he be in the middle of the Terrible Twos? If there were Terrible Twos around, he couldn't see them.

Later that night, wearing his pajamas with teddy bears, after his light was out, he peeked out from under the covers to see if the Terrible Twos were out there. They sounded scary.

They weren't anywhere around, and he was quite certain his mother had been wrong. But he put his pillow over his head, just in case.

"If you would be trained," his mother said, buttoning his overalls, "you would be a big boy. You could dress yourself. You would never be wet. You wouldn't have to have that dumb box of Pampers."

Sam thought about that after he scampered away to play with his blocks. He *liked* that box of Pampers. He could stand on it and reach things. There was a lot of interesting stuff in Anastasia's room, on her desk: crayons, and some chewing gum, and a deck of cards with Ks and Qs, and a brand new goldfish, Frank the Second, in a bowl.

Sam planned to drag his Pampers box into Anastasia's room some day soon, when no one was looking, and stand on it and reach the top of her desk.

He would do his father's desk, too, because his

father had a typewriter, and Sam liked to type stuff.

So it made no sense to Sam at all, when his mother said that about not having to have the box of Pampers anymore. He *needed* that big box of Pampers.

Still, he was fascinated by the idea of being "trained."

Sam knew about trains. He had books about trains. His favorite was *The Little Engine That Could.* Sometimes he made Mom read it to him two times before he went to sleep.

" 'I think I can, I think I can, I think I can,' " he and his mom would say together. Then: " 'I thought I could! I thought I could!' " Sam loved that part best.

So he liked the idea of being trained himself. He stopped saying "no" when his mother sighed and said, "I wish you would be trained, Sam." He began saying "maybe."

He began saying "chugga chugga chugga" when he walked down the hall of the apartment. He was practicing being trained.

One day his mother came home from shopping. Sam was playing on the living room floor while his father watched a baseball game on TV. His father was *supposed* to be watching Sam; before she left, his mother had said, "Myron, will you watch Sam while I do the shopping?" And his father had said, "Sure." But he hadn't *really* watched Sam at all. He watched a baseball game instead.

When his mom came home, she said, "Sam, I brought you a present."

"Animal crackers?" Sam asked. Often she brought him a little box of animal crackers.

"Nope," his mother said. She reached into the bag she was holding and pulled out a little package. "Look! I brought you training pants!"

Sam took the little package and looked at it with interest. Training pants. He hadn't even known that train people wore special pants. Maybe he hadn't looked carefully enough at his favorite book.

He ran to get *The Little Engine That Could.* He sat down on the floor and turned the pages to look at the pictures again. The *train* didn't wear pants. The engineer wore pants, but they weren't white like the pants his mother had bought for him. The train engineer wore a special hat, though. It was striped, blue and white. He wore it on every page except the last, because on the last page, the engineer's hat flew off, right into the air, when the train said, "I thought I could!"

Sam trotted back to the living room, where his dad was still watching baseball.

"I want a training hat," Sam said.

"Ask your mom," Dad said. "She's in the kitchen."

Sam picked up the little package of training pants and went to the kitchen. "I don't want these," he said. "I want a training *hat.*"

His mother sighed. "Look, Sam," she said. Carefully she opened up the package. She took out three pairs of pants. "See? They're just like Daddy's."

Sam looked. They *were* just like Daddy's, only smaller. Sometimes, while Sam watched, his daddy stood in the bathroom and shaved carefully around his beard. Sometimes his daddy wore training pants when he was shaving.

Sometimes his daddy walked down the hall to his bedroom, wearing training pants. But he never said "chugga chugga chugga."

"Don't you want to be like Daddy?" his mother asked.

Sam thought about that. He didn't want to have a beard, especially. He didn't want to watch baseball on TV. He loved his daddy, but he didn't want to be like his daddy, especially.

He wanted to be like the train guy in the book,

and drive an engine, and wear a blue-and-white striped hat.

So Sam said "No" and gave the training pants back to his mother.

She looked exasperated. "Sam," she said, "don't you want to be toilet trained?"

Toilet trained? What did *that* mean? That was the weirdest thing he had ever heard. He wouldn't mind being freight trained. He wouldn't mind being passenger trained. He would *love* being circus trained, like the train in his favorite book.

But *toilet* trained?

"*No,*" said Sam loudly. "*No.* No. No no no no no no."

And his mother began to shriek, just the way Anastasia did. "I CAN'T STAND THE TERRIBLE TWOS!" his mother shrieked.

Sam looked around, but the mysterious Terrible Twos were still invisible.

"I thought I could, I thought I could, I thought I could," Sam sang as he chugga-chugged down the hall.

5

"Sam," Anastasia said in a serious voice, "I have something very important to tell you. Horrible, awful news. You're going to hate it just as much as I do."

"What?" Sam asked. Anastasia had just changed his diapers and now she was trying to snap up his overalls. He liked it better with his legs bare, so he wiggled about.

"Hold still," Anastasia said, "and listen."

Sam stayed very still. He listened.

"We're moving," Anastasia said.

Sam stared at her. She was mistaken. He was being absolutely still. He wasn't moving at all.

"I'm not moving," Sam said.

"Yes, you are," Anastasia said. "We all are. Our whole family."

He continued to stare at her. It was true that she was moving. She was snapping his overalls, and in a minute she would put his sneakers on him, and tie them, which meant that her hands would be moving.

From the kitchen, he could hear his mom's footsteps as she walked from the stove to the refrigerator to the sink. His mom was certainly moving.

He didn't know about Dad. But it was almost the time when Dad would be getting home from atwork, so probably Dad was moving, too.

But Sam was absolutely motionless. So Anastasia was wrong.

"I'm not moving," Sam whispered. He whispered it so that not even his lips would be moving.

Anastasia tied both of his sneakers. She sighed. "Yes, you are," she said mournfully. "You have no choice." She adjusted his overalls, lifted him, and stood him on the floor.

Sam was very still. He tried not even to breathe. "I'm still not moving," he whispered.

"Mom!" Anastasia called toward the kitchen. "Sam's on my side! Sam says that he is absolutely not moving!"

His mother appeared in the doorway. "We'll discuss it later," she said. "Sam? You want to help me frost some cupcakes?"

"Sure," Sam said. He began to breathe again. He ran toward the kitchen. "Now I *am* moving," he called to his sister. "I like moving."

Anastasia glared at him. "Traitor," she said.

Sam loved moving day. Men with tattoos on their arms came in and out of the apartment. Sam had never before seen anyone with tattoos.

One man had a fish, another man had a dragon, and the third had an anchor.

Sam decided that when he grew up, he would be a moving man, so that he could have tattoos. When no one was looking, he took a blue marker and made himself the beginning of a tattoo on one arm. Possibly it was the beginning of a dragon.

The moving men carried everything to their truck. They carried the living room couch. When they picked up the couch, their tattoos bulged.

"Oh, no!" said Sam's mom, after the moving men picked up the couch. "That's disgusting!"

Sam looked where she was pointing. He didn't think it was disgusting at all. He thought it was *wonderful*.

A whole lot of lost stuff appeared on the rug where the couch had been. There were three socks, each covered with gray dust. There was the plastic pretzel that Sam remembered from when he was a baby just getting teeth. There was some green paper, crumpled up. Anastasia grabbed it.

"A dollar!" she said. "Finders keepers!"

That was okay. Sam found four pennies.

"What's *this*?" Mrs. Krupnik asked, with a look on her face that meant "yuck." She poked something with the toe of her sandal.

"I dunno," Anastasia said. "It's something gross."

Sam knew what it was. But he didn't tell them. It was part of a lunch that he hadn't wanted to eat, once, quite a long time ago. Tuna fish sandwich. When he had stuffed it under the couch, he had thought it would disappear forever.

He began to remember all the other things he had hidden in other places. A vitamin pill under the washing machine. A partly chewed cucumber. He had poked that under the radiator in Dad's study.

And broccoli. Sam hated broccoli. Every time they had broccoli for dinner, Sam waited until no one was looking, and he hid his broccoli in his lap or his pocket. Then, later, he tucked it under the corner of the living room rug and squashed it down carefully with his foot. There was a whole year's supply of broccoli there by now. A mountain of broccoli, all squashed. Sam had always thought that he would never get to see it again. He had thought that it had disappeared forever.

Now, on moving day, he waited. The living room rug was one of the very last things. Sam had to wait while the movers did everything else: the beds, the desks, the tables and chairs.

Finally, after all the furniture was in the truck, they returned to the living room. One of them — the one with the blue-and-red dragon tattoo — leaned down to begin to roll the end of the rug.

But Mrs. Krupnik stopped him. "No," she said. "Not the rug."

Sam looked at her in surprise. He wanted very much to see what had happened to his broccoli, especially now that he had seen how his tuna fish sandwich had turned an interesting shade of blue.

"We're leaving the rug here," his mom told the moving man. The man shrugged and dropped the edge of the rug back down on the floor.

"Why?" Sam asked. "Why can't we take the rug?"

"Dad and I bought a new rug for the living room in the new house," his mom said. "We'll leave this one for the people who move in here. They can decide what to do with it."

"Why? Why don't we keep it?"

His mom frowned. She kicked at the rug with her toe. "It's gotten old," she said. "I used to like this rug. The color is so nice. But somehow, it's lost its shape. It doesn't lie flat the way it should. We'll just leave it as a surprise for the next people," she told Sam. "Maybe they'll be really happy to have a free rug."

And broccoli, Sam thought. Lots of free broccoli, too.

The new house was very, very different from the old apartment.

It was much, much bigger.

There were three floors instead of just one. Front stairs and back stairs.

There were lots of rooms. Three bathrooms instead of just one. More closets than Sam could count.

He got lost, looking around. It was scary. He had to stand very still and listen until he could hear the sound of the moving men carrying furniture. Then he had to go down a hall, through a room, and down some stairs to find people.

"Hi, Sam," Anastasia said. "Where were you?"

He couldn't answer because he didn't know where he had been.

"Lost," he whispered and took Anastasia's hand.

She laughed. "I'll show you where your bedroom will be," she said. "Come on."

She took him back up the stairs, down a hall, and into a big empty room with blue wallpaper. A closet door was open, and he could see the huge empty closet, exactly the kind of closet that monsters would live in, Sam was sure.

"Here," Anastasia said. "This will be your room, and you're going to have a real bed, like a big boy, instead of a crib."

Sam put his thumb into his mouth. The room was very, very big. "Not my crib with the clowns painted on it?" he asked in a small voice.

"Nope. You're too big for that now."

"Will your bed be here, too?" he asked his sister, talking carefully around his thumb.

"Nope. My room's on the third floor. I'll show you in a minute. Look here, down the hall. Here's where Mom and Dad will be."

Sam peeked in. He could see that their big bed was already set up. But there was enough room. His bed would fit right beside it. He tugged on Anastasia's jeans.

"I want my bed here, too," he said.

She knelt beside him. "Don't you want your own room?" she asked.

"No," said Sam.

Mrs. Krupnik appeared in the doorway. "What's wrong?" she asked. "Don't you like your room, Sam?"

"No," Sam said.

"Don't you like our new house?"

"No," Sam said.

Mrs. Krupnik sighed. "Anastasia," she said, "I can see that the Terrible Twos are still with us."

Sam looked around nervously. He listened. He could hear a door slam downstairs. He could hear the moving men bumping around with furniture. He could hear his dad's voice, telling them where to put things.

But he couldn't see or hear the Terrible Twos anywhere.

Anastasia pried open the lid of a large cardboard box. "It's going to take us all summer to unpack, Mom," she said. "Look, Sam! It's your trucks!"

Sam looked. His sister lifted out his blue tow truck and put it on the floor. Next came his bright yellow tractor.

"Is my steam shovel there?" he asked. "And my crane? And my front-end loader?"

Anastasia nodded. "All here. Hey, Sam, I have

an idea. Let's dump out all the trucks, and then we'll put the big empty box on its side, to make a garage — down the hall, in your room — and then we can drive the trucks down to their garage, one by one."

"Yeah!" Sam said. "Let's!"

Anastasia set up the cardboard garage in the big blue bedroom down the hall. Then she, and Sam, and Mrs. Krupnik all got onto their hands and knees.

"Rrrrrrrrr," they all said, and began pushing trucks across the bare floors and down the long hall.

Sam's father came up the stairs and stood there watching.

"You can do the fire engine if you want, Dad," Sam said.

So Dr. Krupnik got onto his hands and knees and made a siren noise as he pushed the red fire engine slowly down the hall.

A moving man came to the top of the stairs and watched, wiping the sweat from his forehead, as the Krupnik family crawled in a line along the hall floor.

"Can I do one?" the moving man asked.

"Take the dump truck," Sam directed, and the moving man began to crawl and say "Rrrrrrrrr," also.

Another moving man came up the stairs, looked, laughed, and then got down on his hands and knees with the police rescue vehicle.

The third moving man appeared, looking puzzled, with a can of Pepsi in his hand. He stared at them for a moment. Then he shrugged, put the Pepsi down on the top step, and got himself a truck. He chose the big gray steam shovel. He made it say "Clankety-clank" as he drove it down the hall at the end of the procession.

There were seven people now, crawling slowly down the hall, pushing trucks and making engine and siren noises.

Finally they were all in Sam's big new bedroom: Sam, and his mom and dad, and Anastasia, and all three moving men, sitting on the floor surrounded by trucks.

"Well," said one of the moving men, the one with the tattoo dragon, "next we'll set up your bed, Sam. Right here against this wall be okay?"

Sam looked at the wall where the man was pointing. A few minutes ago the room had looked scary. It had looked too big and too empty and too far away from all the people in his family.

But now, all of a sudden, it looked okay. Now his trucks were lined up on the floor, waiting to drive into the cardboard box garage. Now there was another, unopened box under the window, and he knew what was in it: his blocks. Soon they would bring up his bookcase and the box that held all of his books.

Sam nodded. "Okay," he said to the moving man with the dragon. "You can put my bed right there."

The three moving men got to their feet and headed for the stairs.

"It's not a crib!" Sam called after them, just in case they might have the wrong idea, might think he was still a baby. "It's a *bed*! A real one!"

6

"Sam," said his mom one day after they were settled in the new house, "we're going to do something exciting today. We're going to visit your school. Next month you're going to start school, and today we'll go there to visit."

Sam looked up from his trucks with surprise. "Will I go to Anastasia's school?" he asked.

He wasn't sure he wanted to. Anastasia's school was going to be called junior high, and his sister had confessed to him, "Sam, I am *terrified* about going to junior high."

But his mother said no. Sam would not be going to junior high.

"Will I go to Daddy's school?" Sam asked.

Daddy's school was not called junior high. Daddy's school was called a very complicated name: Harvarduniversity. Daddy had gone to Harvarduniversity a million years ago, when he was young and didn't have a beard. And later he had gone to another school called Yaleuniversity, and later he had gone to *another* school called Columbiauniversity; and now that he was an old guy with a beard, he was back at Harvarduniversity again. Sam had been there to visit Daddy at his office. Daddy's office door had his name on it.

"Can I go to Harvarduniversity? Can I have my name on my door?" Sam asked. "Like Daddy?"

But his mom laughed and said no. Sam would not be going to Harvarduniversity.

She tied Sam's shoe. "Sam," she said, "your shoes are always untied. I think I'll get you some of those sneakers that have fasteners made out of — what is that stuff called, the stuff that sticks together?"

Sam shrugged his shoulders. "I don't know," he said.

"Xerox?" asked his mother. "No, that's not it." She gave him a cookie. "You're going to *nursery* school," she told him.

Sam picked the raisins out of his cookie, to save

them till last, and thought about that. Nursery school.

"Is it Rolex?" his mother asked. She was still thinking about the sneakers. "I think that's it. I'll get you sneakers with Rolex fasteners, so that when you're in nursery school — no, darn it. Rolex isn't right."

Nursery school. Sam thought about it some more. Sam knew about nurses. Every time he went to the doctor, there was a nurse there. She was a pretty nice nurse, and Sam liked her just fine, and sometimes she gave him a lollipop before he went home.

"Spandex?" his mother said. "Lastex?"

Sam wondered if he would wear a uniform at nursery school. He didn't want to wear a white dress, the way the nurse in the doctor's office did. But he liked the idea of a uniform. He would like an army uniform, maybe. Or a Red Sox uniform.

"Lego? No, Lego is that toy," Sam's mom said. "What the heck is that sticky stuff called?"

Sam ignored his mother and continued thinking about the nurse. She *did* give lollipops, that was true. But she did something else, something Sam didn't like to think about very much.

She gave shots.

Sam hated shots.

But now that he thought about it, he liked the

idea of being the guy who gave shots to other people. And after he went to nursery school and learned how, he would be able to do that.

He wasn't sure that he wanted to be a nurse because he still thought he would like to be a mover. And lately he'd been thinking about airplane pilot. But he would go to nursery school anyway, he decided, to learn to give shots.

"Okay," he said to his mom. "Let's go have a look at nursery school."

"Velcro!" his mother said.

Mrs. Krupnik pushed Sam in his stroller to the school. He carried his newest favorite book on his lap — the one with airplane pictures in it. Anastasia had told him that there would be lots of books at nursery school, but he was afraid that there might not be one with airplane pictures.

"I'm not going to *do* anything at the school," he told his mother before they left home. "I'm only going to sit and look at my airplane book."

"Well," said his mom, "that would be okay, I guess. But I'm sure they'll have toys there. I would think you'd like to play with the toys."

"No," said Sam. "I wouldn't."

"And there will be other children, too. Maybe you'd like to play with them."

Sam shivered. He was accustomed to playing by himself at home. He didn't *want* to play with other children. They always grabbed things. And here at nursery school, probably all the children were learning to be nurses, and that meant — oh, *no . . .*

They would have to practice giving shots. They would want to give shots to *him*.

"NO," he said loudly to his mother. "I AM NOT GOING TO GO NEAR THE OTHER CHILDREN."

His mom sighed. "Okay," she said.

Now, as they approached the school, Sam held on very tightly to his airplane book. He could see stuff in the fenced yard. Interesting-looking stuff. A big swing made out of a truck tire. A whole climbing thing painted different colors. A slide shaped like a giraffe. Sam could see that you climbed up the giraffe and slid down its long neck, and that it would probably be a whole lot of fun.

"I'm not going to do that giraffe slide," Sam said to his mother. "I'm only going to do my airplane book."

"Okay," said his mom.

"Even if they *make* me," Sam said. "Even if they tell me I *have* to do the giraffe slide, I'm not going to do it."

"They won't make you. No one will make you do anything."

"Even," Sam said, "if they tell me that they'll hold my airplane book very carefully for me while I do the giraffe slide, I'm not going to do it. I'm going to say, 'You can't make me.' "

His mom lifted him out of the stroller. She folded it into its umbrella shape. "Sam," she said, "I promise you that no one will make you go down that slide."

"Well," said Sam, looking back at the playground as they went through the door, "I might go down the giraffe slide just one time to be polite."

"It's better than junior high, and it's better than Harvarduniversity," Sam announced at dinner, "and it's the best school in the whole world, my school is. There is a slide like a giraffe, and there are a million books, and some of them have airplane pictures, and there are paints that you can moosh around, but you have to put on a smock first. And I'm going to have lots of new friends, and one of them is named Adam."

"That's nice, Sam," said his dad. "Katherine, would you pass the salad?"

"Adam plays rough," Sam said, "and the teacher has to say 'Time Out, Adam!' "

"Go ahead and finish the salad, Myron," Mrs. Krupnik said. "Otherwise, I'll just have to throw it away. Eat your veggies, Sam."

Sam took a bite of string beans. "No uniforms," he announced with his mouth full. "But everybody wears OshKosh, same as me. And there's a dress-up corner," he continued, "with a big box of clothes you can put on. And *hats*. There's a policeman's hat, but if a girl puts it on, then it's a police*woman's* hat, and there's an army helmet, and —"

"Great, Sam," Anastasia said. "Mom, you know what I did today? I —"

"And there's a big Mexican hat, called a somberro," Sam went on.

"*Sombrero,*" his mother corrected.

"Right. Somberro. That's what I said. And my friend Adam put on the somberro —"

"*Sombrero,*" his father said.

"Does anybody want to hear what I did today?" Anastasia asked. "We had an English test, and I —"

"So my friend Adam put on the somberro," Sam continued, "and he took a block from the block area and pretended the block was a gun, and he was aiming it and shooting it, but the teacher took it away and said 'Time Out, Adam.' So then Adam —"

"Sam," said his mother. "Eat."

Sam put a forkful of potato into his mouth. He swallowed it hastily without chewing. "So then Adam took a toy airplane, and he was zooming it around, and he pretended that it was dropping bombs on the cooking corner. That's where the little sink is and the stove, and you can run real water — they let you do that — and you can use an eggbeater in the water and make soapsuds if you want. These other guys, Jeremy and Skipper, they were making soapsuds, and Adam came by and bombed their soapsuds. But the teacher took the airplane away and said to Adam, 'No bombs,' so then Adam —"

"Sam," Anastasia said, "could you be quiet, please?"

"That's what my teacher said," Sam told her, "when it was Quiet Time. We all had to do this." Sam put his fingers to his lips and said "Ziippppp." After demonstrating, he added, "And then our lips were zippered and it was Quiet Time. When it's Quiet Time you can color or look at books, but you *can't* talk or sing or yell for a little while. That's the rules. My friend Adam —"

Anastasia put her fingers to her lips.

Dr. Krupnik put his fingers to his lips.

Mrs. Krupnik put her fingers to her lips.

"Zzzziiipppppp," they all said together.

Sam looked up. He closed his mouth. He was very quiet.

Then he whispered, "And they don't give shots. I love my school."

7

Sam and his mom were at the supermarket. It was one of Sam's favorite places, because he got to ride in the cart with his legs dangling, and he got to point at things.

"I want *that,*" he would say, pointing at bananas. And usually his mom would say, "Okay," and she would put bananas into the shopping cart.

"I want *that,*" Sam would say, pointing to orange juice and to chocolate milk. And those things would go into the shopping cart.

"And I want *that,*" he said, pointing, but he always knew she would shake her head and say no in that aisle. It was the cookies-cakes-candies–

sugary cereal aisle. She always whizzed through that one, pushing the shopping cart very fast, grabbing a bag of flour or some oatmeal, but nothing else.

Sam didn't mind. He waited for the yogurt department and pointed again, because his mom always said yes to yogurt.

Finally, with a very full cart, they got to the check-out line. Sam looked up to see which line they were in. There was one that he hated.

It was the No Candy line.

For a long time, when he was smaller, he hadn't understood about the No Candy line. Then, after he turned two, and then two and a half, and was big and going to nursery school, he began to understand about letters and about reading.

At home, he had plastic alphabet letters that stuck to the refrigerator door. He could spell his name and *Mom* and *Dad.* He couldn't spell his sister's name, but that was because she had a name that was longer than the whole alphabet.

One day he realized he could spell *no.* His mother had found him playing with her jewelry box and trying on her earrings. She had knelt down on the floor, picking up all the necklaces and earrings that he had scattered about. She was very angry.

"No, Sam," she had said in a loud voice. "No, no, N–O, NO!"

Sam listened carefully. *N,* she had said. And *O.* He had both of those letters on the refrigerator. While his mother was still looking for the last of her jewelry, he had scampered away to the kitchen and spelled *NO* on the refrigerator.

Later, his mother had shown him how to spell *yes.* But he liked *no* better.

Not long after that, he had seen the word *No* at the supermarket. It had another word after it, but he didn't know what the other word was. He asked his mom. He pointed to the sign.

"*Candy,* that says," his mom explained. "The sign says, 'No Candy.' If you go through this line, there won't be all those candy bars and things. Some people like this line better. *I* like this line better, as a matter of fact."

Sam scowled. He didn't like the No Candy line at *all.*

And today she was at the No Candy line again. Rats.

"Can I get down and walk?" Sam asked his mom. She was putting the groceries onto the counter so that the woman in the pink smock could drive them over the beeping thing with the green and red light. Usually Sam liked to watch that. But today he wanted to get down.

His mother was counting the yogurts as she took them out of the cart. She nodded. Then, after she had the seven yogurts on the counter, she lifted Sam out of the carriage and down to the floor. "Stay right here," she said. "Don't run off."

"I won't," Sam told her. He had no intention of running off. He was simply going to walk four steps sideways over to the next line, one that had candy bars and things. Just to look.

An old man was there, buying a lot of frozen dinners and toilet paper. He didn't even glance down at Sam. If he had, Sam would have said "Excuse me."

Sam wiggled past the old man and stood in front of the rows of candies. There were all kinds: Hershey bars, gumdrops, chewing gum, licorice. Milk Duds and Chuckles and Baby Ruths and M & M's.

Sam wanted one very badly. It didn't even matter which one.

He looked over at his mother. Her shopping cart was still half full. She was lifting a bag of oranges to the counter. She wasn't watching Sam at all.

He looked up at the old man. The old man had his wallet in his hands and was counting out dollar bills. He wasn't noticing Sam at all.

The lady in the pink smock was putting the old man's frozen dinners into a bag. She didn't even know Sam was there.

Very quietly Sam reached up and took a bright red giant-sized package of Dentyne gum.

Very quietly he put it into his pocket.

He looked around. No one had seen him do it. No one at all.

Quickly Sam scurried back to the No Candy line and stood beside his mother.

"I'm just standing here," he said to her in a loud voice. "I'm not being naughty or anything. I'm not doing anything at all."

She looked down and smiled. "Good," she said. "I'm almost through."

When his mother had paid for the groceries, the lady in the pink smock looked down and said "Have a good day" to Sam.

Sam didn't say anything. He reached for his mother's hand.

He *had* been having a good day. He had had a good morning in nursery school, playing with Adam. He had gone down the giraffe slide headfirst. Nobody had shoved him in line. Nicky, who usually bit everybody, had been absent. He hadn't spilled his juice. He knew all the words to the "Eensy-Weensy Spider" song. He had been the one chosen to put the gray cloudy face on the big calendar today. He had successfully zippered his lips at Quiet Time.

He had had a *very* good day coming home from nursery school in the carpool car. They had had a flat tire. Flat tires were among Sam's very favorite things. And this was an especially good flat tire, because there were seven kids in the carpool station wagon, and four of them started to cry — not Sam, of course. The carpool driver, Skipper's mom, got very flustered and kept telling the kids to zipper their lips, but none of them did.

Sam tried to tell Skipper's mom how to change a flat tire, but she didn't seem to want to listen.

Finally a *police* car had stopped, and a policeman had changed the tire. He made all the kids get out of the station wagon first. He had let Sam squat down very close and watch.

So Sam had had a very good day on the way home from school.

And he had still been having a good day at lunch time, at home. Mom had taken his painting of a rainbow and hung it on the refrigerator with a magnet shaped like a strawberry. He and Mom had had hot dogs. *Peter and the Wolf* was on the radio, and they had listened to it all the way through.

And he had had a good day at the supermarket, pointing at things and helping his mom choose vegetables. She hadn't put broccoli in the shopping cart, only carrots and string beans, Sam's favorites.

But now, suddenly, he wasn't having a good day anymore.

His good day had ended, Sam realized, when he took the bright red giant-sized pack of Dentyne gum and put it into his pocket.

"You're being very quiet, Sam," his mom said on the way home from the store. "Are you tired?"

"No," Sam said in a small voice.

"Is something wrong?" Mom asked.

Sam reached into his pocket and very quietly felt the package of gum. "I'm not having a very good day," he told his mom.

"Oh? Why not?"

A tear slid down Sam's cheek. He pulled his hand, in a fist with the gum inside, out of his pocket. He looked at it and felt all choky.

"Sweetie? What's the matter?" his mom asked.

It was because she said "sweetie." That was the worst. Lots of kids at school cried for dumb reasons: because they didn't get to be first for graham crackers at snack time, or because Nicky bit them, or because the carpool car had a flat tire. Sam *never* cried at things like that. But when your own mother said "sweetie" and you didn't feel like a sweetie at all because you had this bright red giant-sized pack of Dentyne gum in your hand, and you didn't even *like* Dentyne gum, or *want* Dentyne gum, and you weren't having a good day at all, well —

Sam began to sob.

He handed the gum to his mother.

And after they returned to the supermarket, found the manager, explained about the gum, apologized about the gum, paid for the gum, and then went outside and threw the gum away in a big trash can, it began, finally, to be a good day again.

8

"I want a pet," Sam said one evening at dinner.

His mom reached over and patted his cheek. "Oh, Sam," she said, "you know how much we would love to have a dog. But Daddy's allergic to dogs."

"My eyes get all itchy, and I sneeze and feel terrible if I'm anywhere *near* a dog," his dad said. "And I turn grouchy. I snarl at everyone."

"What about —" Sam began.

"Same with cats," his dad said.

"I had a cat once, Sam," Anastasia told him, "when I was younger, before you were born. And Dad was sick for two whole months before we realized it was the cat causing it."

"Was he sneezy?" Sam asked.

"Yes."

"And grumpy?"

"Just like the Seven Dwarfs," Anastasia said.

"Did you have to *kill* the cat?" Sam asked. He sort of hoped they had. He didn't want anybody's cat to be dead, especially, but for some reason he was very interested in shooting guns and dropping bombs. At nursery school, Sam and his friend Adam always dropped a lot of bombs on stuff until the teacher said, "Time Out, guys," and made them stop. Now Sam was kind of wondering about how you would get rid of a cat that was turning you into a Sneezy and a Grumpy. Maybe you would have to drop a bomb on it.

"Of course not," Anastasia said. "We gave the cat to my friend Jenny. Later it got run over by a car."

"Squooshed flat?" asked Sam.

"Yuck," Anastasia said. "I suppose so. But I don't want to think about it while I'm eating."

"Eat your dinner, Sam," his mom said. "Chicken's your favorite."

"Could I maybe have an *alive* chicken?" Sam asked. "I really want a pet."

"No, sweetie. People raise chickens on farms. I think your school is going to have a field trip to a real farm some time soon. So you'll get to see lots of live chickens. But you won't be able to keep one, I'm afraid. A chicken wouldn't be a good pet, anyway."

Sam scowled and drove his spoon around his plate, pushing a trail through some peas into a mound of squash. Oh, yuck. Now there were some peas touching his squash. He hated when his foods touched each other. The *worst* was when spinach juice got onto mashed potatoes and turned them green.

No. The *real* worst was when *beets* touched something.

Sam poked at his peas. "Anastasia got to have gerbils," he grumbled.

The whole family groaned. Sam giggled. The gerbils had been terrible. They had had babies, and then they had all gotten out of the cage, and there had been gerbils all over the house for a while.

The Krupniks had all been very glad when they finally gave the gerbils away.

Carefully Sam removed three peas from his squash mound and tried to de-squash them with his finger. It didn't work. No one was looking at him, so he put the squashy peas into his pocket. He could throw them away later.

He gnawed on his chicken leg and wished that he could have a pet. If he had a pet, it would be sitting under his chair right now, right this minute. And he could drop peas down and his pet would eat them and no one would ever know but Sam. A good pet would even eat *broccoli,* Sam thought.

"You stay in the yard, Sam," his mom said. "And after I finish the dishes, I'll bring you in for your bath. It's almost bedtime." She buttoned his sweater.

Sam nodded. His mom closed the screen door, went back into the kitchen, and left Sam alone on the back porch. It was boring, being outdoors after dinner. There were no kids around. At school, there would be lots of kids yelling and shoving and grabbing and running. Nicky would be biting people, and Adam would be dropping bombs on the castles that other kids would be building in the sandbox, and Skipper would be going down the giraffe slide headfirst, and it would be a whole lot of fun.

But being alone in the back yard was boring. Sam sat for a minute on his tricycle. He pushed the pedals with his feet, rode the tricycle into a bush, got off, and left it there, mashing the rhododendron.

He watched a squirrel climb the side of a tree tunk. Squirrels couldn't be pets; they always ran away very fast if you came close. A pet should be willing to sit beside you, eat your peas, and listen quietly while your mom read you a story. A squirrel wouldn't do any of those things.

He wandered over to his sandbox, sat down on the triangular corner seat, and reached for a big spoon that was partly buried in the sand and dirt.

When he picked it up, he saw a worm.

Sam wasn't afraid of worms. Sam wasn't afraid of *anything* much, except maybe the Terrible Twos, which he *still* had never seen. And Nicky at school, who bit, and left little pink circles of teeth marks on your arm.

But he had never thought very much about worms until now. He picked this one up and examined it. It was long and fat and glistening, and it wiggled in the palm of his hand.

Could a worm be a pet? Sam wondered. He had never heard of anyone who had a pet worm. But maybe no one had thought of it yet.

A worm was small, the way a pet should be.

It was alive.

No one was allergic to worms. He was pretty

sure of that. Daddy was allergic to dogs and cats. Sam's friend Adam was allergic to orange juice, so at snack time at school Adam always had tomato juice instead. And Sam's mother was allergic to ironing; he had heard her say that lots of times.

But no one was ever allergic to worms, Sam was quite sure.

And a worm would never surprise you by having lots of babies the way Anastasia's gerbils had. Worms didn't have babies. In his whole entire life, Sam had never once seen a baby worm.

A worm would never ever run out into the street and get squooshed flat by a car the way a cat might. Because worms didn't have legs. Sam lifted the worm and dangled it in the air, checking. No legs.

And Sam thought of something else good about worms. Sometimes, when they were walking to the store, his mom would grab Sam's hand and say, "Watch out. Dog mess." Sam would have to walk very carefully around it.

But she never once said, "Worm mess." So that was *another* thing that worms didn't do and another problem that a pet worm wouldn't be.

A worm would sit quietly beside you while your mom read a story, Sam was sure. This worm was sitting quietly in his hand right now.

Would a worm eat peas? Or broccoli? Probably not. Sam wasn't even sure that a worm had a mouth. He held this one up and examined each end of it carefully. There were things that *might* be a mouth, but he wasn't certain.

But he was certain of something: it wouldn't bark or whine. That would certainly please his parents, who didn't like barking and whining one bit. There was a dog across the street — Mr. Fosburgh's poodle, Clarence, who barked and whined a lot — and sometimes Mrs. Krupnik said that she wished Mr. Fosburgh would move to Australia and take Clarence with him.

"Saaaammmm!" He could hear his mother call him from the kitchen door. It was time to go in for his bath.

"I'm coming!" Sam called back. Carefully he rolled his worm into a ball and put it into his pocket, where it would have three peas to eat just in case it was hungry, just in case it *did* have a mouth, just in case it was willing to eat peas.

Trotting to the house, he tried to think of a name for his new pet. He had wanted to have a dog and name it Prince. But he had named one of Anastasia's gerbils Prince, so that name was taken, even though they didn't have the gerbil anymore.

What was a *better* name than Prince?

King, Sam thought, with satisfaction. He grinned, climbing the porch steps. He patted his pocket.

King of Worms, he thought.

9

Sam was at the public library with his sister and his mother late one afternoon. The public library was one of his very favorite places.

He liked to call it the *liberry,* even though everybody — his mom, his dad, his sister, and the librarian herself — had all told him about a million times that *liberry* was wrong. He knew that. He knew it was really *library*.

So he said it correctly, aloud. But to himself, Sam always said "liberry." He liked the sound of it better.

Sometimes on Saturdays, the librarian showed children's movies. *The Red Balloon* was the one that Sam liked best. It had no scary parts at all.

Winnie-the-Pooh was pretty good, too, but Sam always got a little nervous when Pooh was up in the air, dangling from the balloon, and bees came along. Sam was just a teensy-weensy bit frightened of bees.

After he had chosen his books, and the librarian had checked them out, Sam went to the bulletin board by the library's front door. He wanted to see if they would be having a movie soon. He looked all over the bulletin board for a picture of Dumbo, or Bambi, or Willy Wonka.

None of those things was there.

But Sam *did* see a sheet of pink paper with some drawings of dogs and cats. They weren't very good drawings, but you could tell they were dogs and cats.

And there were some words on the paper.

Sam screwed up his face and began to sound out the letters.

P was easy. "P, p, p," Sam sounded in a whisper.

And "T, t, t," he said.

"Pet," Sam read aloud.

Then he started on the second word. Sam knew that "Sh" was the sound of being quiet, and the second word began with "Sh."

"Pet Shhhhh," Sam said quietly. He looked at the next letter. An *O*.

"PET SHOW!" Sam yelled.

Everyone in the library turned to look at him. A man with a newspaper scowled, but most people smiled.

"That's right, Sam," the librarian said. "We're having a pet show for children on Saturday morning. With *prizes.* Do you have a pet to bring?"

Anastasia was at the counter, checking out *Gone With the Wind* for the fourteenth time. "You can't take my goldfish," she said hastily. "Frank the Second is not one bit interested in being exhibited."

"I'm afraid he doesn't have a pet," Mrs. Krupnik said to the librarian in a sad voice. "My husband is allerg——"

"I do!" Sam said. "I do! I didn't tell you! It was a secret!"

Back at home, he raced up the stairs to his room, with his mother and sister behind him. He opened his closet door, pushed aside the boots and sneakers and slippers on the floor, and found the little box he had hidden in the corner.

His mother was looking very nervous. "Sam, what do you have in there? If it's a snake or something, I really don't think I can —"

Sam took off the lid. "Shhh," he said. "He may be asleep."

"Yuck," Anastasia said, peering into the box. "It's just *dirt.*"

"No, no, it's *in* the dirt! Look! I'll find him!" Carefully Sam poked through the dirt until he found his pet. "Here he is! His name is King of Worms!" Sam held the earthworm in the air.

His mother and sister stared at it. They didn't say anything.

"I could tie a ribbon around him for the pet show," Sam suggested.

"Yeah, right," said Anastasia. "Cute."

"I have to get dinner started," Mrs. Krupnik said. "Sam, be sure to wash your hands carefully after you put your, uh, your pet away. Anastasia, make sure he washes, would you?"

Anastasia nodded.

"Funny," Mrs. Krupnik murmured as she headed down the stairs. "I was going to cook spaghetti for dinner. But now I've changed my mind."

Anastasia walked with Sam to the public library on Saturday morning. Their mother and father had decided to stay at home.

"Dad would have liked to come," Anastasia

told Sam, "but you know with his allergies, he was worried about being around dogs and cats."

Sam nodded. He was carrying his worm box very carefully.

"And Mom was afraid there might be rodents," Anastasia said.

"Yeah. Mom hates rodents."

They both remembered how much their mother had hated Anastasia's gerbils.

"Good thing a worm isn't a rodent," Sam said, patting his box. "Mom likes worms okay."

"And fish," Anastasia added, thinking of Frank.

They were almost at the corner, where the small brick library building was set in the middle of a big green lawn. The pet show would be on the library lawn, under the trees.

Sam could hear the sound of barking.

"A *dog* won't win first prize," he said confidently to his sister, "because dogs are ordinary."

"Let me tie your shoe tighter, Sam," Anastasia said suddenly.

She knelt on the sidewalk, and Sam looked at her in surprise. "Nobody needs to tie my shoes," he reminded her, "because Mom bought me Xerox shoes. I mean Velcro," he corrected himself.

"I really only wanted to talk to you for a minute," Anastasia explained, as she knelt beside him. "Sam," she said, "don't be disappointed if you don't win the prize. Prizes don't matter."

"Yeah, they *do*!" Sam told her. "Prize means *best*. I think King of Worms will be the best pet! I washed him. And I changed his dirt."

"But, Sam, *every* child thinks his pet is the best. And we don't really care what the judges think, do we? As long as *we* know King of Worms is the best, that's the important thing, isn't it?"

Sam shook his head. "No," he said. "The really important thing is to win the prize."

Anastasia sighed. "Come on," she said. She stood up and took Sam's hand, the hand that wasn't holding the worm box. "Let's get it over with."

The library lawn was very noisy. Dogs were barking, babies were crying, children were shouting — Sam recognized some of his nursery school friends — and a lot of people were standing around a tree, looking up and calling to a cat, asking it please to come down.

The librarian recognized Sam and Anastasia. She gave Sam a number on a square of cardboard. "There you are," she said. "Your pet is number seventeen. And your place will be over there. Do you see the seventeen on that table? Better get in your place because the judging will start soon. Then we'll have refreshments, afterward."

Anastasia nudged Sam over to the empty card table with the 17 taped to it. They placed the little box on the center of the table and removed the lid.

Sam poked gently in the fresh dirt until he found King of Worms. "Stick your head out," he whispered, "and look beautiful when the judges come around."

"Hey, look, Sam," Anastasia said, "somebody *did* bring a goldfish. See over there?"

They checked to make certain that Sam's worm box was safely situated on its table, and then wandered over to look at the goldfish in a bowl nearby.

"Not as good as Frank the Second," Anastasia whispered to Sam, and Sam nodded in agreement. "Not as bright-colored, not as big. And Frank's face is more intelligent."

Sam tugged suddenly on Anastasia's jeans. He pointed. "That's Nicky from my school," he whispered. "Remember Nicky the biter?"

"Well, Nicky wouldn't dare bite anyone at a pet show," Anastasia reassured Sam. They strolled over and looked into the huge box beside Nicky.

"Forty-seven gerbils," Nicky said in a loud voice.

"Nice," Anastasia said politely, and she and Sam moved away.

"And there's my friend Adam with his cat." Sam pointed. "Adam's cat is named Squeaky."

"Shhh," Anastasia said. "Look. There are the judges!"

The three men and one woman were stopping in front of the first pet, a rabbit in a cage, and discussing it. Sam could see them talking quietly to each other. One man was carrying a shopping bag. He reached into it and took out a bright blue ribbon with a badge attached to it. He wrote something on the badge and attached it to the rabbit's cage. The girl standing beside the cage grinned proudly.

"No fair!" wailed Sam. "They're giving the prize and they didn't even look at King of Worms!"

The judges had moved on to the next pet. Anastasia grabbed Sam's hand, and they ran over to the rabbit cage.

"I won!" the girl was saying happily. "My rabbit won!"

Anastasia read the words on the blue ribbon. "First Prize," she read aloud, "for Nose-wiggling."

Sam brightened. "King of Worms couldn't win that," he said, "because he doesn't have a nose."

"Look, Sam," Anastasia said. She had moved to the next pet. The judges had gone on ahead, moving from table to table, cage to cage.

"First Prize for Yellowest Pet," Anastasia read, leaning over a canary cage.

"First Prize for Largest Sleeper," she read, almost tripping over a snoring Newfoundland dog.

"First Prize for Wettest Pet," she read on the goldfish bowl.

"First Prize for Best Climber," she read on the ribbon attached to a tree trunk. From a limb above, the cat still looked down.

"First Prize for Most Pets," said the award on Nicky's huge box of gerbils.

Sam and Anastasia stood and watched quietly from a distance as the judges came to the table with the 17 on it. They saw the judges lean over the worm box.

"Maybe he'll be roundest pet," Anastasia suggested.

"I bet he'll be dirtiest," Sam said cheerfully.

They could see the judges poke gently in the dirt. One of them lifted the box. They talked some more.

"They can't decide," Anastasia whispered to Sam. "It must be a truly tough decision."

"They probably never had to do a worm before," Sam whispered back.

Finally, while they watched, the judge with the marking pen wrote on one of the blue ribbons and attached it to the worm box. Then the judges moved on.

Sam and Anastasia dashed to their table.

"Read it to me," Sam begged. "I can't read fast enough because I have to sound out all the words."

Anastasia had the ribbon in her hand and a horrified look on her face.

"First Prize," she read slowly, "for Most Invisible Pet."

And it was true. King of Worms was gone.

"He's bait!" Sam yowled. "I know he's bait!"

"What on earth are you talking about, Sam?" Anastasia asked. They were walking home from the pet show.

Sam couldn't stop crying. "King of Worms! I know there must have been someone there who wanted to go fishing tomorrow! And was looking for bait! And they saw King of Worms and *took* him!"

Anastasia leaned over and held a crumpled Kleenex to Sam's nose. "Here," she said. "Blow."

Sam blew his nose. "They'll put a *hook* through him," he wailed.

Anastasia shook her head. "I don't think so, Sam. I think he ran away. He just didn't want to be in a pet show."

"Worms can't run," Sam muttered. "They only crawl."

"Well, that's true. They crawl and slither. But that makes them very good at escaping."

"Why?" Sam asked.

"Because they go underground, and no one can see them. Hey, Sam, you know what? I bet King of Worms is underground right now, maybe right under our feet."

Sam sniffled, and his face brightened. "You think so? Under the sidewalk?"

"Sure," Anastasia said. "Probably slithering along down there, faster than a speeding bullet. Heading home."

Sam looked down the street, toward their house. "Probably he did want to go home, so he wouldn't have to be in a dumb pet show," he said. "Would he know the way home? Because I took him in the box, and he couldn't see anything."

"Oh, sure," his sister told him. "Worms have an excellent sense of direction. They're used to finding their way underground, where they can't see."

"Yeah," said Sam, starting to smile. "I bet he's slithering under the street right now. He doesn't even have to stop at the corner and look both ways for cars."

"He'll probably beat us home," Anastasia said.

At the corner, they stopped. Sam looked down at the drain that caught the rainwater. He knelt beside it and cupped his hands around his mouth.

"Hey, King of Worms!" he called. "I know you're down there!"

He listened for a moment. "I think I hear him," he said to Anastasia. "I hear slithering noises."

When they got to their yard, they went directly to the sandbox where Sam's big tin shovel was lying beside a dented kitchen pot.

"Where do you think he might be, Sam?" asked Anastasia.

Sam thought and then pointed. "Right here," he said. "By this bush."

Anastasia dug very carefully with Sam's shovel. Sure enough, just a few inches below the surface, they found King of Worms.

"He beat us home," Sam said happily. "He should have won First Prize for Fastest Slitherer."

10

"It's Monday, Sam," Mrs. Krupnik said at breakfast. "Show-and-Tell day at nursery school. Are you going to take your blue ribbon from the pet show?"

"Nope," Sam said, dragging his spoon through his oatmeal. He liked the way he could open up a ditch and then watch it fill gradually with milk. Sometimes he made Drowning Men out of raisins.

"Why not?" Anastasia asked.

"*Because,*" Sam explained impatiently, "Nicky will be there with a dumb blue ribbon for Most Pets. And Adam will bring his First Prize for Cat with Fattest Tail. *Everybody* will be doing pet show stuff at Show-and-Tell today."

"Oh," said his mother. "I hadn't thought of that. But you're absolutely right."

"What *are* you going to take?" Anastasia asked.

"Secret," said Sam.

But he was fibbing. It wasn't a secret at all. The truth was, Sam couldn't think of anything to take to school for Show-and-Tell. He had this problem almost every single Monday morning.

Sam was good at a lot of stuff. He could count higher and recognize more words than any other kid at nursery school. He knew more songs than almost anybody; he even knew all the words to the songs on his father's Billie Holiday records. (Sam especially liked the part that went, "I get no kick from champagne, Mere alcohol doesn't thrill me at all"; he always sang that part very loud, even though his parents said, "What will the neighbors think?")

And he was good at somersaults, and coloring, and building very tall castles out of blocks, and bashing the castles to the ground afterward.

But he just wasn't any good at all at Show-and-Tell.

Other kids were. A girl named Rosie had brought, one Monday, her new baby brother to

Show-and-Tell. Of course her mother had to come along; but Rosie got to hold the baby all by herself, in front of the other kids. She got to tell the baby's name — Henry — and when Henry cried, she let all the other kids look into his mouth, so they could see how he had no teeth.

A kid named Kevin had brought things back from a trip to Disney World and took up almost the whole Show-and-Tell time, wearing his Donald Duck hat and telling about the rides and stuff. Kevin had official pilot wings that he got on the airplane; he had them pinned to his sweater, and he wouldn't let the other kids wear them, not even for one minute.

Every Monday, Sam worried about what the other kids would bring to Show-and-Tell. And what he would bring. Nothing he had ever brought seemed to be very good.

Today, after he had finished his oatmeal, he went back up to his bedroom to look around.

There was nothing there but the same old stuff: same old toys, same old books, same old clothes. He didn't even have his pet worm anymore. He and Anastasia had decided that King of Worms probably liked living outdoors, underground, better than in a box in Sam's closet.

Sam wandered down the hall into his parents'

bedroom. Maybe *they* had something that would be interesting at Show-and-Tell.

"Sam!" his mother called from downstairs. "Do you have your jacket on? Your carpool will be here in a few minutes!"

"Yes," Sam called back. "I'm coming!"

He looked around. His father's pajamas were on the floor.

Sam imagined himself standing in front of the circle of children at nursery school, holding up big striped pants with a drawstring at the waist. "These are my daddy's pajamas," he imagined himself saying.

No. That was no good. Probably *everybody's* daddy had big striped pajamas.

He looked around some more. On the table beside the bed was something that belonged to his father. Sam picked it up.

"Sam!" his mother called from downstairs. "Time to go! Your ride is here!"

Sam put his Show-and-Tell surprise into the pocket of his jacket. He headed for the stairs. Then he turned back, grabbed something else that was on the table, and put that into his other pocket.

He ran downstairs, kissed his mother goodbye, and headed off to the waiting station wagon.

*

It was Circle Time. Skipper had pasted a fat smiling yellow sun on the calendar's Monday, and Mrs. Bennett had played "You Are My Sunshine" on the piano while all the children sang. Altogether, they had stood in the circle and said the Pled Jelly-juntz. "I pled jelly-juntz to the flag," Sam had said in his most grown-up voice, with his hand over his heart. His other hand was in the pocket of his jeans, holding on to his secret for Show-and-Tell.

Everyone called "Me! Me!" when Mrs. Bennett said, "Who has something for Show-and-Tell today?"

Mrs. Bennett looked around the circle and said, "Let's let Amy go first. Amy?"

Sam made a face. He didn't like Amy much. She had a long ponytail, which was perfect for pulling, especially if she flipped it around right in front of your face. But if you pulled it, Amy cried and told on you.

Amy stood, flipped her long ponytail, and held up a postcard. "My grandma sent me this," she said. "From Florida."

Everybody stared politely at the picture of a palm tree. "*My* grandma sent *me* a postcard from Florida," Rosie said, "and it had an *alligator* on it."

"I saw a real alligator at the zoo!" Adam yelled. "*Two* alligators I saw!"

All the children began making alligators out of their hands, snapping them like big jaws, grabbing each other's sleeves and pulling fiercely, the way they imagined real alligators would.

Sam didn't. Sam was still holding his surprise inside his pocket.

"Thank you, Amy," Mrs. Bennett said. "That's a lovely postcard. Quiet, children! No more alligators, please! Who's next? Leah? How about you? Do you and Rollie have something to show us today?"

Leah nodded her head shyly, and Mrs. Bennett pushed her to the center of the circle. Rollie was Leah's wheelchair. Once, when Leah first started school, her mother had been there with her. Her mother had lifted Leah out of the wheelchair and held her on her lap, so that each of the other children could have a turn in Rollie.

Sam hoped that Leah's Show-and-Tell would be that everybody could try Rollie again.

But Leah put her finger to her lips and said, "Shhh. Everybody be quiet so you can hear what I learned to do. Zip your lips."

Everybody zipped their lips, even Sam. He had to let go of his secret in order to zip his lips.

When they were all very still, Leah took a deep

breath and swallowed. Then she gave an enormous burp. She grinned.

"Fake burp," Leah said. "My daddy taught me."

All of the children forgot that their lips were zipped. They shrieked with laughter.

"Do it again!" Sam called, and Leah did it again, very loudly.

"Show us how! Show us how!" The kids were calling all together.

So Leah sat up very straight in her wheelchair and gave burping lessons. Fake burping wasn't easy. Skipper finally managed a pretty good one, but most of the children simply giggled and sputtered, and Nicky got the hiccups.

Mrs. Bennett was the most successful at it. She did a huge loud fake burp on her second try, and everybody clapped.

"Okay," Mrs. Bennett said, laughing. "Time for just one more person before we go out to the playground." She looked around the circle.

"Sam," she announced. "Your turn."

Sam stood up. He knew his was better than the palm tree postcard. But the fake burps — well, it would be tough to be more interesting than fake burps.

He took his father's pipe out of his pocket and

put the stem of it into his mouth. Then he took the lighter out of his other pocket and tried to push hard on the little ridged wheel that would make the flame appear. All of the children were watching in amazement.

"HOLD IT!" said Mrs. Bennett in a loud voice. "Stop right there, Sam Krupnik. What on earth are you doing?"

That was a strange question, Sam thought. Anybody could *see* he was lighting a pipe. But he took the pipe out of his mouth and explained to his teacher.

"I'm lighting my pipe. I'm showing how I smoke my pipe."

"Not in this nursery school, you're not. I'm ashamed of you, Sam. Does your father know that you took his pipe?"

Sam hadn't even thought about that. When he took the pipe, he'd been thinking about being interesting at Show-and-Tell. He hadn't thought of it as taking. As *stealing*.

He wished he had been the one to do fake burps instead of Leah. He wished Mrs. Bennett's angry face would go away.

"It's not my daddy's pipe," Sam said. "It's *my* pipe. My daddy has a different pipe. We sit around and smoke our pipes together at home."

"Oh?" Mrs. Bennett said. He could tell that she didn't believe him.

"And my mom and my sister, they both smoke big cigars," Sam added. His voice was a little quavery. It was quavery because he was lying. But he couldn't seem to stop.

Mrs. Bennett took the pipe and the lighter from Sam. She knelt beside him and put her arm around his waist. Sam felt terrible. All the kids were staring.

"I'm *very* glad Sam decided to give us all a lesson about health and safety," Mrs. Bennett said. "You taught us all an important thing, Sam."

"I did?"

"You certainly did. We all need to be reminded about how dangerous fire can be, right?"

"Right," said Sam.

"And we should never, *ever* play with lighters or matches?"

"No," Sam said in a loud voice. "Don't anybody *ever* play with lighters or matches!"

"And what do we think about smoking?"

"YUCK!" Sam shouted. The kids in the circle all clapped their hands and yelled "YUCK!"

Sam looked around and grinned. He was being a bigger hit than Leah.

Mrs. Bennett kept the pipe and the lighter. She

said she would send them back to Sam's father with the carpool driver.

Sam decided, as he was putting on his jacket for the playground, that when he got home he would have a serious talk with his mom and daddy and Anastasia, too, about safety and health. He would also teach them how to do fake burps.

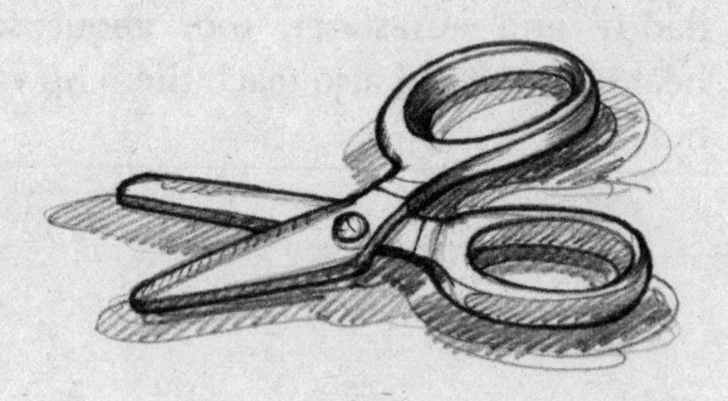

11

Sam sat on Anastasia's bed and watched his sister brush her hair. Anastasia had long hair and every night she tried to brush it, she had told Sam, one hundred strokes.

"Eighty-two, eighty-three, eighty-four," Anastasia was saying softly as she brushed.

"A hundred and forty-nine," Sam said loudly.

Anastasia stopped brushing and glared at him. "Don't, Sam," she said. "You'll get me all mixed up."

He waited quietly until she got to one hundred and put the brush down.

"Now do me," he said.

"Your hair looks fine," Anastasia said. "You don't have oily hair like I do."

"I just have dumb curls," Sam muttered.

"You have *great* curls, Sam. I'd give anything to have curls like yours. In fact, you know what? I'll tell you a secret."

"What?" Sam asked. He loved secrets.

"Well," his sister confided, "when I was younger, I used to be jealous of you. Sometimes when people would come to visit Mom and Dad, they would all start talking about what pretty curls the baby had."

"What baby?" Sam asked.

"You, when you were little. When people started talking about how cute you were and what pretty curls you had, I would get so jealous and mad that I would leave the room. I would go sulk."

"Did you cry?"

"No, of course not," Anastasia said. Then she added, "Well, sometimes I did. Once or twice."

Sam sighed. "I was such a cute baby," he said with satisfaction. "Very, very, very cute."

He raised himself to his knees so that he could look across the room into Anastasia's mirror. He frowned at himself. "Now I hate my curls," he said. "I wish I had punk hair."

"Punk hair?"

"Yeah. My friend Adam has punk hair. His hair all sticks up like a porkypine."

"Porcupine," Anastasia corrected him automatically. "Is it dyed orange or green or anything?"

"No, it's just a plain brown porkypine. And he has a little tail at the back." Sam felt the back of his own head. "I wish I had a little tail like Adam."

"Well," Anastasia said, "I think it's very weird for a three-year-old kid to have a punk haircut. When you're *big,* you can get one if you want to. Although to be honest with you, I think it would freak Mom and Dad out if you did."

Sam grinned. He pictured his mom and dad freaking out. They would probably scream and faint. Maybe ambulances would have to come, with their sirens going. He would stand there with his punk haircut and direct the ambulance people and tell them what to do.

"Sam, would you go downstairs, please? I have to do my homework now," Anastasia said. "I can't concentrate when you're fooling around in my room."

"I'll go if you give me five brushes. You don't have to do a hundred."

So Anastasia picked up her hairbrush again, brushed Sam's curls carefully five times, and patted him on his behind fondly. "You're still cute, Sam," she told him.

"Yeah, but I have these dumb curls," Sam said glumly. He left his sister's room.

Sam could hear his parents talking quietly downstairs. He could hear the television news in the background. If he went down to where they were, they would make him be quiet while they watched the news and talked.

He wandered into the bathroom instead. If he stood on the closed toilet seat, he could open the medicine cabinet, and there was interesting stuff in there.

First he took out his dad's shaving cream and pushed the button on top so that it foamed out into his hand.

He smeared it on the bottom of his face so that he had a beard. Then he closed the medicine cabinet and leaned over so that he could see his white-bearded face in the mirror.

Sam giggled.

Still wearing his foam beard, he opened the cabinet again. This time he noticed his mother's perfume. He sprayed it across his chest and sniffed.

Next, he thought he would try the hairspray.

But as he reached for it, he noticed the small pair of scissors that his father used to trim his beard.

Sam wondered if you could trim a *foam* beard. He fitted his fingers into the scissors handles and tried.

But it didn't work very well. Part of his beard fell into the sink.

He closed the mirrored door again and looked at himself to see if his beard was still okay, even if a piece of it had fallen off.

But when he looked, he found himself looking more at his hair than at his beard. He found himself looking at his curls. His dumb curls.

Very carefully he reached up with the scissors and snipped at a curl. It fell into the sink on top of the foam. Where the curl had been, there was now just a small tuft of hair. It was sticking up. Straight up.

He stared at it. It was the beginning, he realized, of a punk haircut.

He snipped another curl and watched it drop into the sink.

And another.

He began to wonder whether, when he finished the top, he would be able to figure out how to make the little tail in the back.

He snipped again.

*

Lime

Twenty minutes later, through the closed bathroom door, Sam could hear his mother's footsteps coming up the stairs. He could hear her voice.

"Anastasia?" she was saying. "Sam? It's awfully quiet up here. What are you guys doing?"

"Homework," Sam could hear his sister call.

Sam put his scissors down. He looked around the bathroom. The beard foam had dissolved and was mostly gone. But there was hair everywhere.

"Is Sam in your room?" he heard his mother ask.

"No, he went downstairs a long time ago," Anastasia replied.

"Sam?" his mother called.

Sam leaned over the sink and looked once more into the mirror. Foam had dried on his chin and cheeks, and snippets of hair had dried in it, so he had a fuzzy beard. His curls were mostly gone. Here and there a curl remained, but most of his head was — well, it wasn't what he had hoped.

He had hoped for little tufts and spikes, like Adam's hair, and a small tail in the back.

But something had gone wrong. It was chunks. And there was a bald spot right in front. He hadn't wanted a bald spot at all.

"Are you in the bathroom, Sam?" His mother's voice was louder.

He looked at himself again. The head looking back at him didn't look like Sam Krupnik at all.

"No," he called. "Someone else is in the bathroom."

His mother knocked on the door. "I beg your pardon?" she said.

"Are you looking for your cute little boy, Sam?" Sam called nervously.

His mother chuckled. "Yes, I am," she called through the door. "It's his cute little bedtime."

"Well," Sam replied very slowly, "Sam has disappeared. He turned into someone else, I think."

His mother opened the door. She opened her mouth, as if she were going to say something, but no words came out. She stared.

"I'm not Sam anymore," Sam whispered miserably.

His mother's mouth remained open, but she didn't speak.

"I'm a porkypine," Sam wailed. "An *ugly* one!"

For a very, very long moment his mother still said nothing. They stared at each other in absolute silence.

"Sam," she said at last, "I have never *ever* wished to have a porcupine instead of a son."

"I know," Sam said, sniffling.

"And for the very first time, I feel a terrible desire to spank you," his mother said. "An urge — an almost uncontrollable urge — to spank you. A *need* to spank you."

Sam poked out his tongue to catch a tear that was coming down his sticky cheek. He tasted hair and dried foam.

"I don't think," his mother continued, "that I am actually *going* to spank you. But I want you to know that I would *like* to."

Sam nodded. "Me too," he said miserably. "I want to spank myself."

"Do you think," his mother asked, "that we could try to laugh, instead?"

"I don't feel like laughing," Sam said, spitting out some stray bits of hair.

"Neither do I," said his mom. "But here are the choices. You could cry. I could spank you. If I spank you, then *I* will cry, too. Or we could both laugh."

"Let's try to laugh," Sam said sadly.

"Ha ha," they both said, and turned the corners of their mouths up very slightly.

Sam's lower lip was still quavering. He laughed again. So did his mom. At first it wasn't easy. But after a moment, the laughter was real. It got louder and louder. Anastasia came running in to see what was going on. Sam's father came upstairs with the newspaper in his hand.

For a very long time, all four Krupniks stayed in the small bathroom together. Sam's father was sitting on the edge of the tub. Sam was still standing on the closed toilet seat. His mother and sister leaned against the wall where the towels hung.

They howled with laughter. They laughed until they were exhausted.

The next morning, bright and early, Sam went with his mother to the barber for repairs. For four weeks, until his curls grew back, he had the most interesting punk hairdo in town. It was even better than his friend Adam's.

12

"Katherine," Sam's daddy said at dinner, "this is terrific fish chowder."

"Thanks," said Sam's mother. "It *is* good, isn't it? It's fattening, though. All that cream."

Sam looked up from his own chowder. He liked it because he could mash up crackers in it, which was fun. But he wasn't thinking about his chowder. He was thinking about something that he had just noticed for the first time.

"Why," Sam asked his father in a thoughtful voice, "do you call Mommy 'Katherine'? But I call her Mommy?"

"Well," Dr. Krupnik explained, "I can't call

her Mommy because she s not my mother. My mother was named Ruth."

"Did you call her Ruth?" asked Sam.

"No, I called her Mother. But her name was Ruth."

"What was your daddy's name?"

Sam's father grinned. "His name was Sam. Like you. That's why we named you Sam when you were born. It was Anastasia's idea."

Sam frowned. It was all very puzzling. "But why do you call me Sam? I know my name is Sam. But your name is Myron, and I don't call you that. If I call you Daddy, why don't you call me Son? And why don't you call Mommy Wife?"

His father said, "Well, I suppose I could do that." He looked at Mrs. Krupnik and said, "Could I have another helping of chowder, please, Wife?"

"Of course, Husband," Mrs. Krupnik said, and she took his bowl to the stove where the pot of chowder was. "Would you like some more, Son? How about you, Daughter?"

Sam and Anastasia both said "No, thank you" and giggled.

It was all very confusing, Sam thought, as he finished his dinner.

Anyway, what he *really* wished — he hadn't

told them this — was that they would call him He-Man.

Sam had daydreams about being bigger. Not only bigger, but also stronger and more powerful. He wanted to be someone who could catch criminals, beat up bad guys, fly airplanes, shoot rockets, and end up being He-Man of the Whole World.

All the guys at Sam's nursery school wanted the same thing. Their favorite games had to do with blasting off and zooming and bashing. They were so noisy that Mrs. Bennett was always saying, "Time Out, guys," and then they would listen to her read a story about Babar or Madeline or Curious George.

Sam loved listening to stories. And sometimes he liked to play the quiet games. He liked playing house with Leah and Rosie and Skipper when they would cook pretend dinners on the little stove and serve the dinners to the stuffed animals that they propped up in chairs.

But sometimes, while playing house, Sam would have an urge to race around with the pretend dinner in its plastic dish, and bomb the animals instead of feeding them nicely.

Then Rosie would always start to cry, and Mrs. Bennett would have to say, "Time Out, Sam."

Time Out meant that he had to sit quietly in the big green chair.

Sometimes Sam had Time Out several times every morning. He didn't mind that. Football players had Time Out, too; he saw it on TV when his daddy watched the Patriots.

"Why do they have Time Out?" Sam asked his daddy. "Were they bad?"

"No, they just need to take a rest and to *think* a little bit," his daddy explained.

So that's what Sam did, too, at school, when Mrs. Bennett said "Time Out," and Sam had to sit in the green chair. He rested and thought.

Mostly, he thought about being a He-Man.

"Do I have big muscles?" Sam asked Anastasia. He had pushed up the sleeve of his shirt, and he showed her the top of his arm.

Anastasia was busy with a school project. She was at her desk, with her feet wrapped around the rungs of the chair, and a pencil tip in her mouth. She glanced over at Sam.

"No, I wouldn't say so," she said. "Your arms are kind of skinny."

Sam stuck out his lower lip. "Well," he asked her, "how can I *get* big muscles?"

Anastasia glanced over again, impatiently. "You have to pump iron," she said. "There's this guy at the junior high, Ben Fraser, who has *humungous* muscles. And he got them by pumping iron."

"How can I —" Sam began.

But Anastasia interrupted him. "Sam," she said, "I'm busy. *Please* quit bothering me, okay?"

Sam sighed and wandered away from Anastasia's bedroom. He went downstairs. He thought about pumping iron.

He knew what an iron was. His mother had one. She kept it in the pantry on a shelf, with its cord all twisted around it. His mom was allergic to the iron, she said.

Sam went to the pantry and lifted the iron down very carefully from its place. He took it up to his room.

Then he went to his mother's closet. He kicked aside her sandals and her torn sneakers on the closet floor. He crawled inside the closet and looked around. He saw a couple of old pink slippers. Those weren't what he wanted.

Finally he found what he was looking for, inside a shoebox stacked with others in a corner of the closet. They were high-heeled and black. There were two of them. Pumps.

He took one of the black pumps to his room and laid it carefully on his bed beside the iron.

Then he tried to figure out how to do it. How to pump iron.

But it was a mystery. He could do it *backward.* He could iron the pump. He did that for a while, but it was boring, and it didn't make big muscles at all.

But he simply couldn't figure out how to pump the iron.

Maybe there was another way. Sam went to his mother and asked her. She was in the big studio where she painted, and she was working at her easel, humming and holding a paintbrush with a blue-daubed end in her hand.

"Hi, Sam," she said. "What's up?"

"Do you know how to make big muscles on someone?"

"Well," said Sam's mom, "if I were making a picture of a person, and wanted to make big muscles, I would do it like this." She pulled out a large sheet of paper, drew a man very quickly with a marking pen, and then added a fat bulge on each of his arms. "See?" she said. "Big muscles."

Sam looked. The picture looked a little like Popeye.

"Yeah," he said, "but if it was a real person, not just a *picture* person, how would he get big muscles? How did Popeye get his big muscles?"

His mother laughed. "Spinach, of course. Don't you remember how Popeye gobbles spinach every time he needs more strength and bigger muscles?"

Of *course.* Sam did remember.

And he remembered something else. He remembered that there was some leftover spinach in the refrigerator.

Sam didn't like leftover, cold spinach very much. But he went to the refrigerator anyway, took out the dish that held the spinach, and ate some.

Yuck. It tasted awful.

He checked his muscles. No change.

Another big bite. YUCK.

And he checked again. Still no muscles.

Sam sighed and reached for the bowl of spinach one more time, just as the back door opened. His father was home.

"What are you eating, Sam?" Daddy asked. He set his briefcase down, came over to the table where Sam was sitting, and peered into the bowl. "It looks like cold spinach."

"It *is* cold spinach," Sam said with his mouth full.

"Do you mind if I ask *why* you are eating something so disgusting? Especially when there's good stuff in the refrigerator, like — let's see — apples?"

"I need big muscles," Sam said.

"You do?" his daddy asked. "Why?"

Sam thought about that. "If I had big muscles," he said at last, "Nicky would never ever bite me at school. And no monster would ever dare to come live in my closet. I could chase bad guys. And everybody would call me He-Man."

"Well," his dad said, "I guess that's true. But why are you eating cold spinach?"

"This is how Popeye gets his big muscles."

Sam's daddy sat down. "I'd forgotten that, Sam, but you're right. That *is* how Popeye gets his muscles. And when I was a kid, I tried to get them the same way. But you know what?"

"What?" Sam asked gloomily, reaching for another bite of yucko cold spinach.

"It doesn't work for regular people, only for Popeye."

"It doesn't?" Slowly Sam put the spinach back into the bowl.

"Nope. I thought I'd better tell you before you gave yourself a spinach stomachache."

"But how did you get your big muscles?"

"Me? I don't have big muscles. I'm Mister Flabbo," said Sam's father. "Feel." He guided Sam's hand to the top of his arm, and Sam poked. Through his father's jacket, the arm felt pudgy and soft.

"Anyway," his father said, "you don't want to be like Popeye. He wears terrible clothes."

Sam thought about Popeye's clothes. "They're not so bad," he told his father. "He wears a sailor suit."

"I happen to know, Sam, that your mother bought you a sailor suit. And you absolutely refused to wear it. Remember that day when you were supposed to go to a birthday party, and Mom tried to get you to wear the sai——"

"Yeah," Sam muttered. It was a day he had tried to forget. He had behaved very badly. So, in Sam's opinion, had his mother.

"And *another* thing about Popeye —" Sam's father went on. "I *know* you'll hate this!"

"What?"

"He smokes a pipe."

"That's right!" Sam said. "Just like *you*! Even though Mom and Anastasia and I always always tell you to quit, and Anastasia brought home all those booklets from the American Long Sausage Nation."

"American Lung Association," his father corrected him, with a guilty look. "And I *am* going to quit, I really am. Very, very soon. Probably next week. Or if not next week, the week after that, for *sure*."

Sam's daddy looked so unhappy that Sam reached over and stroked his arm to let him know that he loved him, even if he *did* smoke a pipe.

"Good old Mr. Flabbo," Sam said. "I love you."

"Thanks, Sam," his daddy said. "I love you, too. Let's you and I start doing some exercises together, so we can work on the old muscles."

Sam grinned. He put the bowl of spinach back in the refrigerator. "Come on," he said to his daddy. "Let's go pump iron."

13

Sam slithered on his belly up the stairs and into his sister's bedroom. Her door was partly closed, so he slithered in very carefully through the open part, making no noise.

Slither, slither, slither.

Anastasia didn't see him. She was on her bed, writing in her notebook.

Anastasia was *always* writing in her notebook.

"It's my private notebook," she had told Sam. "And don't you ever dare peek into it. Because I have ways of knowing if you do."

"What ways?" Sam asked. "I could do it while you're at school, and you would never, ever know." (Anastasia never took the private notebook to school.)

"Yes, I would. Sometimes I put an invisible hair across the cover, and if the hair is dislodged I know a spy has been into my notebook."

"Lemme see. I want to see the invisible hair," Sam had said.

But Anastasia had said no. "Just keep your mitts off of it," she told him. "People my age — thirteen — have private stuff, and they don't want their little brothers messing around with it."

"People *my* age have private stuff, too," Sam had told her.

He didn't, really. Didn't have any private stuff. But he liked to try to make himself invisible, which was a way of being very private, and that was why he was slithering invisibly into Anastasia's room.

"BOO!" Sam shouted, leaping up suddenly, beside his sister's bed.

Anastasia jumped, startled. She dropped her marking pen.

"Sam!" she said in an irritated voice. "Cut it out. You scared me. What are you doing, creeping around like that?"

"I'm being a lizard," Sam explained.

Anastasia laughed. "Well, you make a pretty good lizard, Sam. Why don't you slither downstairs and eat some insects? That's what lizards do. Go out in the yard and find a nice juicy caterpillar for lunch, okay?"

Sam thought about that. He thought about a huge, fuzzy, juicy caterpillar, placed right in the center of a piece of whole-wheat bread, maybe with a little mustard dabbed on him.

Suddenly Sam didn't want to be a lizard anymore, not even for one minute longer.

"Will you play with me?" he asked Anastasia. "I'm not a lizard anymore. I'm a boy again."

Anastasia looked up from her notebook. "I will a little later, Sam. We can go outside and I'll give you a ride on the back of my bike, okay? But not right now. Right now I'm making up a secret code, and I need to do it all by myself, without any interruption."

Sam's eyes widened. "What's a secret code?" he asked.

"Oh, it's complicated, Sam. It's when you say one thing but mean something else. Or *write* one thing but mean something else. Understand?"

Sam shook his head no.

"Well, for example . . ." Anastasia hesitated. "Sam," she asked, "if I explain this code to you, promise me you won't tell anyone?"

Sam nodded.

"Do you solemnly swear?"

Sam gulped. He knew that swears were bad.

There was a kid at nursery school who was always saying swears, and Mrs. Bennett did not find it amusing *at all,* not even for one single minute. (It was Sam's best friend, Adam.)

"I solemnly swear," Sam whispered, glancing around to be certain no one could hear.

"Well," Anastasia explained, "I've made a list of all the boys I know. Robert Giannini and Steve Harvey and Eddie Fox and — well, all the boys I know. See?" She tilted the notebook so that Sam could see a list of names written in green ink.

"Now, here's the code part," Anastasia went on. "I've written words after each boy's name, but the words don't really mean what they say. So if I wrote *love,* that really means 'hate,' see? And *despise* means 'love'. And my friend Meredith has the code, too, so she can understand. And if I call Meredith up and say, 'I despise Steve Harvey' — well, Meredith could look at her code notebook and see that would really mean that I *love* Steve Harvey. But no one else would know, because they wouldn't know the code."

Sam stared at his sister.

"See?" Anastasia asked.

"I guess so," said Sam, even though he didn't, really.

"Don't forget that you can't tell anyone. You solemnly swore, remember?"

"Yeah." Already Sam was sorry that he had solemnly sworn. It hadn't been worth it. He dropped to his belly and slithered out of Anastasia's room and down the stairs. He was a new kind of lizard: a kind that didn't eat bugs, only peanut butter.

"What were you doing upstairs?" asked Mrs. Krupnik, as Sam ate his sandwich. He had slithered into the kitchen, explained about the peanut-butter-eating lizard, and his mother had realized that it was probably feeding time in the lizard world.

"I learned about code," Sam told her.

"Code?" his mother asked, wrinkling her forehead.

"Yeah, that's when you say one thing but you really mean something else."

"Like what?"

Sam sighed. He couldn't tell about Anastasia's code because he had solemnly sworn. But suddenly he thought of something else.

"Like Mr. Flabbo," he said. "If I said Mr. Flabbo, you know who I would mean, don't you?"

His mother laughed. "Sure. You'd mean Daddy."

"Right. Because Mr. Flabbo is code for Daddy. And if I said, 'I hate Mr. Flabbo,' it would *really* mean 'I love Daddy.' "

"Oh." His mother looked confused.

Sam looked around the kitchen. On the floor in front of the washing machine there was a huge stack of dirty clothes. He recognized the shirt he had worn yesterday, and he recognized the chocolate milk he had spilled on that shirt at dinner last night. He saw Anastasia's socks and his dad's pajamas. He knew how his mother felt about laundry.

"If you said, 'I love doing the laundry,' " Sam explained, "that would be code, and it would *really* mean —" He waited for his mother to catch on.

She laughed and sipped her coffee. "I guess I see. But I hope you won't say you hate anything, even in code, Sam. Okay? Because *hate* is such a yucky word. Even for laundry."

Sam nibbled out the rest of the good part of his sandwich and arranged the crust in an O on his plate. "Yeah, okay," he said. Actually, he didn't think *hate* was a yucky word. *Broccoli* was much yuckier.

Sam went outside and wandered across the yard to visit the Krupniks' next-door neighbor. Her real name was Gertrude Stein. But Sam never called her that. He liked to call her Gertrustein.

Gertrustein was very old. Sam wasn't sure how old, maybe two hundred.

She had a grouchy face, and when Sam had seen her for the first time, he had been frightened by her face. But later, when he got to know Gertrustein, when they became good friends, he realized that she was actually a smiling sort of person. But her skin had drooped, so it hung down in a grouchy look, and sometimes it was hard to see the smile underneath.

Gertrustein was on her back porch, hanging a dishtowel on the clothesline there. She always moved very slowly. Her arms and legs ached all the time, she had explained to Sam, and that was why she moved so slowly.

"Hi, Sam!" Gertrustein said when Sam came up the steps. "What a nice surprise!"

She lived all alone. She had no husband, no children, no grandchildren, and no dog or cat. So she was always glad to see Sam.

"If I didn't have you to talk to," she had once told Sam, "I would probably forget how to talk."

Sam thought it was the saddest thing in the whole world, to have drooping skin that gave you a grouchy face, to have aching arms and legs so that you had to move slowly, and to live all alone so that you might forget how to talk.

But Gertrustein didn't seem to mind. Almost every day she made cookies.

"I expect you might be willing to do me a favor and eat a cookie or two," she said to Sam.

"I might," Sam agreed.

"What have you been doing today?" she asked him after they had sat down together at her kitchen table with a plate of cookies and a glass of milk each.

Sam sighed. "Anastasia won't play with me because she's busy writing a code," he said. "And my mom is doing the laundry so *she* can't play with me right now, and she didn't understand about codes, anyway.

"Do you know about codes?" he asked, looking up at Gertrustein. "If I said, 'I don't want another cookie,' it would *really* mean, 'I *do* want another cookie' because it would be a code."

Gertrustein passed the cookies to Sam, and he took another.

"I know a code," she said.

"Do you really?" Sam asked. "Or are you talking in code? Because if you're talking in code and you say, 'I know a code,' then it would really mean 'I *don't* know a code.' "

Gertrustein chuckled. "No, actually, I do know a real code. Not a made-up one like Anastasia's. I know the Morse code. I learned it during the war. I wonder if I can remember it."

She closed her eyes, thinking. Sam sneaked his hand over to the cookie plate while her eyes were closed.

"Dit dah," Gertrustein said aloud.

Sam stared at her.

"Dah dit dit dit," she said with her eyes still closed. "Dah dit dah dit."

Quietly Sam pulled his sneaking hand back, away from the cookie plate. He slid off his chair. He decided that he would escape through the back door, run home faster than a speeding bullet, and tell his mother that something was seriously wrong with Gertrustein. His mother could call an ambulance.

But as he was tiptoeing across the kitchen toward the door, Gertrustein opened her eyes.

"I remember it! Every bit of the Morse code! Let me find a flashlight, and I'll show you!"

That night, after Sam was bathed and in his pajamas and had brushed his teeth and had had his bedtime story and had kissed everyone good night and been tucked in and his light was turned out, he decided that he didn't even need his night-light, for the very first time.

"Are you sure?" his mother asked. "You've *always* had your Mickey Mouse night-light."

"Tonight I don't want it," Sam said firmly. His mother leaned down to where Mickey lived in the electrical outlet on Sam's bedroom wall. She clicked Mickey off.

"Do you want me to leave your door open so you'll have a little light from the hall?" his mom asked.

"Nope," Sam said. So she said good night and closed his door.

His room was very, very dark. After a moment, when Sam's eyes adjusted to the dark, he could see the two big windows and the dark sky outside and a few stars.

He reached under the covers and found his daddy's flashlight where he had hidden it.

Then he tiptoed, carrying the flashlight to his window.

He balanced the flashlight on the windowsill, aimed it across the dark yard, and with his thumb, Sam found the button that would turn it on.

Dit dah dit dah, Sam flashed. That meant: Desire to establish contact.

He and Gertrustein had studied Morse code all afternoon. Gertrustein had said that Sam had a mind like a steel trap. Sam pictured the inside of his own head, shiny steel with springs and teeth like a bear trap, grabbing at the Morse code and holding it tight so it would never escape.

Dit dah dit dah, he flashed again, remembering the signal he had learned with his bear-trap mind. He waited. He knew how slowly she walked, and how long it took her to do things with her aching arms and legs.

After a minute, across the yard, from the upstairs window of the next house, he saw her answer. *Dah dah dah dah dah,* she flashed. Contact established.

Sam grinned in the dark. *Dit dit dit dit; dit dit,* he flashed. Hi. It was very easy to do hi in Morse code. Probably even someone who *didn't* have a bear-trap mind could do it.

Hi, Gertrustein flashed back.

Sam and Gertrustein had decided that they would flash "Hi" to each other every night for the rest of their lives.

She had taught him other messages, too. *Dit dit dit; dah dah dah; dit dit dit* was the one they would use only in case of emergency. If Sam happened to see scary monsters, for example, he could flash *dit dit dit; dah dah dah; dit dit dit* to Gertrustein, and she would save him. She would save him the very next *instant,* she promised.

If Gertrustein fell and broke her aching leg in

fourteen pieces, she needed only to flash *dit dit dit; dah dah dah; dit dit dit* to Sam. He would rescue her in no more than thirty-two seconds, he had promised.

Sam watched through the dark, but there were no more flashes. Only the "Hi." No emergencies, no accidents, no monsters. Gertrustein was safe. So was Sam.

Content, he crept back through the dark room and climbed into his bed again. Carefully he aimed the flashlight at his ceiling and tapped out one more message with his thumb. A private message only for himself. *Dit dit dit; dit dah; dah dah,* he said to the ceiling. That meant *Sam.*

Dit dit dit; dit dah; dah dah, he flashed to the closet where occasionally there might be monsters. Sam. Any monsters would understand what that meant, and that they should go away.

Dit dit dit; dit dah; dah dah, he flashed to the Mickey Mouse night-light. Sam. Mickey would understand what that meant: that he wouldn't be needed anymore.

Dit dit dit; dit dah; dah dah, he flashed to his trucks in their cardboard garage. To the little box of dirt where King of Worms had once lived. To his books. To his jeans in a heap on the chair. To his sneakers with their Velcro fasteners on the floor. And to a half-eaten egg salad sandwich that he had hidden behind the curtains just last week.

Sam, he flashed.

Sam.

Sam.

Sam.

That's *me,* he thought with satisfaction, and he fell asleep.

Read more about
the hilarious adventures of
Anastasia
and her adorable brother, Sam!

Now on sale from Yearling Books
wherever paperbacks are sold.

ISBN: 0-440-40852-0

Anastasia Krupnik

To Anastasia Krupnik, being ten is very confusing. For one thing, she has this awful teacher who can't understand why Anastasia doesn't use capital letters or punctuation in her poems. Then there's Washburn Cummings, a very interesting sixth-grade boy who doesn't even know Anastasia's alive. Even her parents have become difficult. They insist she visit her ninety-two-year-old grandmother, who can never remember Anastasia's name. On top of all that, they're going to have a baby—at their age! It's enough to make a kid want to do something terrible. If she didn't have her secret green notebook to write in, Anastasia might never make it to her eleventh birthday.

ISBN: 0-440-40100-3

Anastasia's Chosen Career

Anastasia Krupnik has exactly one week to work on her school assignment called "My Chosen Career." Determined to be a bookstore owner, she must first develop poise and self-confidence. So Anastasia takes the plunge and spends her life savings on a modeling course at Studio Charmante.

She has one week to interview a bookstore owner, write a report, and complete her modeling course. Luckily, her new friend Henry is with her most of the way. Is Anastasia destined to be a successful bookstore owner or a glamorous model? Only Anastasia has the answers!

ISBN: 0-440-40291-3

Anastasia on Her Own

Help! Anastasia Krupnik's mother must organize her chaotic life. So Anastasia, who is a very organized person, and her father invent the solution to Mrs. Krupnik's problem: the Krupnik Nonsexist Housekeeping Schedule.

But when Mrs. Krupnik goes to California on a ten-day business trip, Anastasia finds that the problem isn't solved at all. It's hard to stick to a schedule that doesn't leave room for her little brother, Sam, who's come down with the chicken pox, and her father's former girlfriend, who's invited herself to dinner. How is Anastasia supposed to cope with these interruptions when she's planning her first dream-date dinner for Steve Harvey?

It's a cinch. As long as she sticks to the Krupnik Romantic Dinner Week Schedule, what could possibly go wrong?

ISBN: 0-440-40087-2

Anastasia Has the Answers

Humiliated. That's how Anastasia feels whenever she tries to climb the ropes in gym class. How come everyone else can climb those hateful ropes?

Since Anastasia has decided to become a journalist, it should be easy for her to answer most questions. Then why can't she understand about Daphne Bellingham's parents' divorce? And why can't she please Ms. Willoughby in gym class?

Finally Anastasia thinks she has the answers! When a team of foreign educators visits her school, she plans a big surprise that will amaze her classmates, Ms. Willoughby, and the visitors.

ISBN: 0-440-40221-2

All About Sam

Everyone knows Sam Krupnik. He's Anastasia's pesky but lovable younger brother.

This is Sam's big chance to tell things exactly the way he sees them. He has his own ideas about haircuts, nursery school, getting shots, and not eating broccoli. Sam thinks a lot about being bigger and stronger, about secret codes and show-and-tell.

Make way for your little brother, Anastasia. Here for the first time is Sam Krupnik's story. What a life!

ISBN: 0-440-40816-4

Attaboy, Sam!

Sam Krupnik is at it again. This time he wants to make a special surprise perfume for his mother's birthday. First he has to collect his mother's favorite smells in Ziploc bags. He uses an old grape juice bottle to hold everything from chicken soup to his father's pipe to a poop-smelling tissue from a baby's room.

Sam stashes all the smells in his toybox and won't let his mother into his room. It's really starting to stink in there. Still, Sam can't wait for his mother to see and smell her birthday surprise. But Mrs. Krupnik isn't the only one who's in for a surprise.